Seventy Stories and a Poem

Seventy Stories
And a Poem

Robert Harris

.: Virtual**Salt**
Publishing
Tustin

To Marie
Wife and Best Friend
Helper and Companion
And Fan of My Stories

Table of Contents

A Note on the Text

The stories here were written over a period of many years. The first 45 stories were written between about 1970 and 1992, when they were published as *Stories From the Old Attic*. The next dozen or so were written between about 1992 and 2011; they were published as *Stories From the Castle Keep* (along with the *Old Attic* stories) on my Web site, www.virtualsalt.com.

The remaining stories are newly written, but they are based on story ideas dating back to as early as the 70s. When I just recently came across a 70-page file of notes and ideas, I thought it was time to cement at least a few more in print and share them with you.

THE SECOND GREATEST COMMANDMENT

A man was out shoveling the excess gravel off his driveway and into the graveled road that ran by his house. A neighbor happened to be walking by just as the man tossed a shovel full down the road the opposite way the man used to drive in and out. "I see you aren't messing up the part of the road you use," sneered the neighbor.

A few minutes later another neighbor happened by and saw the man toss a shovel full of gravel down the other part of the road. "I see you are fixing only the part of the road you use, and not the part others must use," sneered the second neighbor.

The shoveler stood still with a shovel full of gravel as the second man left. Now unsure of what to do with it that would be agreeable to his neighbors, he decided simply to dump it out onto his driveway on the very spot whence he had scooped it up. Just as he did so, a third neighbor happened to be walking by. "I see you are stealing gravel from the road for your driveway," sneered the third man. "People like you are what's wrong with this country."

At this point the homeowner put his shovel away and sat down with his pipe to contemplate these occurrences. Pretty soon a neighbor from further down the street drove by and saw the man sitting down enjoying his pipe. "If you weren't so lazy, you'd shovel some of that gravel off your driveway and back onto the road where it belongs," the driver sneered as he drove away, spinning his tires and scattering gravel in every direction.

✠✠✠

A GOOD HORSE AND A BETTER

A man once came upon a lad about midday skipping stones across a pond. "Hello, young man," he said, approaching. "What brings you here on a school day?"

"I wrote a poem yesterday which was the best in class, and the teacher said I could play today while the other children wrote more poems."

"Well, then, you are to be congratulated. Yours is certainly a deed of distinction. And as a reward," he added, settling himself on a tree stump, "let me tell you a story about two horses."

"Oh, yes, do," the youth said eagerly, sitting down at the man's feet.

"The first horse lived in Arabia, and he was beautiful and strong. He had never lost a race. And he was shrewd. He would run just hard enough to pull away from the other horses in the race, and then he would let up and trot, or even walk, across the finish line, to the great embarrassment and humiliation of all the other horses."

"He was clearly a superior animal," the young poet interjected.

"Yes, he was," agreed the man. "Now the other horse lived in Macedonia, and he, too, was strong and noble. He had, however, lost one race, the first race of his life; and some say he always remembered that when he ran."

"How grating to the heart it must be to lose so early and have a blight on one's reputation," mused the young man.

"But this horse always won every other race. And unlike our first horse, when this Macedonian horse ran and knew he had beaten the other horses, instead of letting up he redoubled his efforts and ran even harder—as hard as he could—for he now ran not against the fortuitous competitors with whom he began the race, but against his own heart: against all horses past and all horses future, against every horse in Macedonia and every one in Arabia, and also against the ideal horse with a pace so frighteningly fast that few can conceive its possibility. And even more than this, he ran toward the perfection of excellence itself. And when he crossed the finish line, as happy as he was to win, he secretly lamented that his opponents had not been fast enough to threaten him and push him onward."

"Even though he lost once," the lad remarked after a short silence, "perhaps this horse was as good as the Arabian."

"Perhaps so, my child," said the man, with a smile. "Perhaps so."

✠✠✠

IT'S NUT VALUABLE

Once upon a time a wise and thoughtful craftsman made a new electric adding machine. It was very complex with many gears and levers and wheels, and it did amazing things, always adding up the numbers correctly. So the craftsman sold it to a businessman for many thousands of dollars. All the parts inside the new adding machine felt good about being so valuable. They worked hard and happily all day, and often talked about how useful they were to the businessman.

But one day a spring noticed a little nut just sitting on the end of a shaft. The spring pulled at the lever he was attached to and pointed. Soon the whole works knew. "You lazy little nut," said a spinning gear, "why don't you get to work?"

"But I am working," said the nut. "Holding on is my job."

"That's stupid," yelled a cam. "I don't believe our maker put you here. You just sneaked in to steal some of our glory. Why don't you get out?"

"Well," said the nut, "I'm sure our maker knew what he was doing, and that I do serve a purpose. I hold on as tightly as I can." But all the machinery began to squeal and abuse the nut so violently that he felt very sad and began to doubt himself. "Maybe I am useless," he thought. He appealed to the shaft he was threaded onto.

"Look, kid," the shaft told him, "I've got plenty of other parts holding on to me. I shouldn't have to support you, too."

So finally the little nut decided to unscrew himself and

go away. He dropped off the shaft and fell through a hole in the bottom of the machine. "Good riddance," said the motor.

"Yeah, good riddance," all the other parts agreed.

Rather quickly the nut was forgotten and things went on as they had for awhile. But in a few hours, the shaft began to feel funny. At first he began to vibrate. Then he started sliding and slipping. He called for help to the other parts attached to him, but they could do nothing. Presently the shaft fell completely out of his mounting hole, causing many levers and gears and cams to slip out of alignment and crash against each other, and forcing the whole machine to grind to a halt with an awful noise. The motor tried his best to keep things going—he tried so hard that he bent many of the parts—and then as he tried even harder, he burned himself out. "This is all the fault of that little nut," the ruined parts all agreed.

"I'll give ya three bucks for it," said the junk man to the office manager.

✠✠✠

STEWARDSHIP

A wise man approached three young men standing around idly. "Here is a coin worth a hundred dollars," the wise man said to the first youth. "What should I do with it?"

"Give it to me," he said at once.

"Rather than reward such selfishness and greed," responded the wise man, "it would be better to throw the money into the sea." And with this, the wise man threw the coin into the water. "Now," he said to the second youth, "here is another coin. What should I do with it?"

The second youth, feeling shrewd, answered, "Throw it into the sea."

But the wise man said, "That would be a careless waste. To follow a bad example only because it is an example is folly. Better than throwing this money away would be to give it to the poor." And he gave the money to a beggar sitting nearby. "I have one last coin," the wise man went on, talking to the third youth. "What shall I do with it?"

The third youth had been paying attention, and, thinking he would get the money if he avoided the greed and wastefulness implied in the answers of his friends, said, "Why, give it to the poor."

"That is a very wise and kind answer," said the wise man, smiling. And because you have answered so well" (at this the youth brightened with expectation), "I will indeed take your good advice and give the money to the poor."

"Don't I get anything for my wisdom?" demanded the

youth.

"You have already received something much better than money," said the wise man.

✠✠✠

THE MAN WHO BELIEVED IN MIRACLES

Once upon a time a traveler arrived in a land quite like our own, full of modern technology like cars and computers and whistling teapots, but with these two differences: there were no television sets and no airplanes. In fact, nothing at all had ever been seen in the sky, not even a bird, and the only movies the people ever saw were in the theaters.

The traveler stayed for about a month on the eastern shore where he had arrived, and then decided to visit the western cities. He mentioned his decision one evening at a meeting of the principal scientists and educators of the region, who had gathered to hear of his travels. Someone mentioned that the west had much to offer, but that the journey between the two areas was unpleasant, consisting of crossing a hot, empty desert. "In that case," said the traveler, "I'll just fly."

"Is that like sleep?" one of the scientists asked.

"No, no," the traveler replied. "You know, fly through the air, like a bird."

"And what is a bird?" someone asked. And so the traveler began to explain about flight and what an airplane was and how it flew from one place to another. The room became very quiet, and the expressions on the faces of everyone present darkened.

"Does he expect us to believe this?" one man whispered to another.

"Well, you know what liars travelers are," someone else added. Finally the host spoke up, slightly embarrassed and slightly indignant.

"If this is your idea of a joke," he began, but was interrupted by the surprised traveler.

"Why, it's no joke at all. People fly all the time."

"I am sorry that you so much underestimate the intelligence and learning of your audience," said a professor across the table. "That a person could enter some metal device—like a car with fins—and rise into the air, and be sustained there, and move forward, why that clearly violates everything we know about the law of gravity and the laws of physics. If we have learned anything from a thousand years of study of the natural world, it is that an object heavier than air must return immediately to earth when it is tossed into the sky."

"Hear, hear," two or three people muttered.

"Now, if you perhaps mean that these 'airplanes,' as you call them, are somehow flung into the air for a short distance and then fall to the ground, well, then perhaps that would be possible." The professor looked expectantly and a bit condescendingly at the traveler, hoping that the man would take this face-saving opportunity.

"No, no. You don't understand," said the traveler. "The airplanes have powerful motors and the craft rise into the air, and they stay up as long as they want, as long as the fuel holds out." There were several audible "hmmphs" around the room.

"Tell us then," said another scholar, in a saccharine voice, "how this device works. What makes it fly?"

"Well, I don't know exactly how it works. It has something to do with air flowing over the wings."

"You don't know—you cannot explain—how it works, this device that runs counter to everything we know about the natural world, yet you believe in it anyway."

"Believe in it?" asked the traveler, a bit confused by this turn of phrase. "Of course I 'believe in it.' I fly on one all the time at home."

"And how do you control its motions?" a man asked, without removing his pipe. The audience was clearly beginning to patronize the traveler, and he was growing a little irritated.

"Oh, I don't control it. There's a pilot for that."

"I see," the pipe smoker said. "So this airplane contains both you and the pilot. You're telling us that perhaps four or five hundred pounds of dead weight can travel through the air as long as it wants."

"As long as the fuel holds out," added one of the hmmphers, with amusement.

"And all the time sneering at the law of gravity and laughing science in the face," someone else noted.

"Well, actually, the planes are much larger than that," said the traveler. "Many of them hold two or three hundred people and weigh, my, I don't know—many thousands of pounds."

"I think we have heard enough," the now-fully-embarrassed and half-angered host said. "It was amusing for awhile, but it's time to put an end to this nonsense."

"It is not nonsense," the traveler protested. "It is the truth."

"Then you really believe this madman's drivel you've been feeding us?" the host asked, rather hotly.

"Of course. How can I not believe it? I see it and live it every day. And here," he added, remembering something, "I even have a photograph."

"Obviously faked," said the host, dismissing it after a glance.

"Who invited this charlatan?" someone asked of no one in particular.

"I thought science had put an end to all this miraculous event stuff long ago," said another man, rising from his chair and preparing to leave.

"Well, let's not pursue this pointless discussion," the

host said. "Our guest apparently knows nothing of science, and is impervious to logic and to the considered opinion of the best minds of our nation. There's nothing left to do but adjourn." The meeting began to break up, and the traveler was putting on his coat when the man with the pipe made one last attempt to reason with him.

"We are all scientists here, all educated men. All of us agree that it is impossible for a heavier-than-air device to fly on its own through the air. Don't you see that? This is against the laws of nature—it violates the law of gravity."

"Well," said the traveler, "perhaps there is another law, or perhaps there is a higher law than the law of gravity, which, when it is understood, will explain how planes can fly."

"That's just what I'd expect a religious fanatic to say," said a man who had been listening in. "Science can jump into the trash as far as you religious types are concerned."

"Not at all," said the traveler. "But your science is not perfect. You do not yet know everything about everything, what is possible and what is not possible."

"Go take your religion to a church and keep it away from serious people," the man concluded, stomping out of the room.

In the weeks that followed, the traveler was ridiculed and denounced in the newspapers, being called everything from a con artist to a prospective mental patient. (The scientific journals said nothing about the man because they considered the whole matter as beneath serious thought.) As a result, the traveler was often left to himself, and so he pulled out his tiny portable television set and began to watch it. Just by chance, some visitors happened to come by and see the little box. They were very impressed and urged the traveler to market his invention for putting a movie inside such a small space.

In a few days, word had spread about this mini-movie

and several scientists were convinced (after some debate) to come see it, together with some engineers representing the movie projector manufacturers of the nation.

They were sufficiently impressed as they watched a few scenes, but when the traveler changed channels, their enthusiasm turned to gaping astonishment. The traveler switched all around, showing them twenty channels in all. Such was the amazement and even incredulity of the engineers that they already began to suspect some kind of trick. The scientists looked confused.

"You certainly have a lot of films stored in that little box," one of the engineers said. "How do you get them all in there?"

"The pictures are not in the box," said the traveler. "They are all over in the air around us. This antenna brings them in and the set makes them visible." The engineers laughed while the scientists sneered, the latter now sorry they had allowed themselves to be talked into coming to hear this notorious nut.

"Come now," one of the scientists said. "Do you expect us to believe that there are pictures floating around us in the air—pictures we cannot see? And that twenty sets of these pictures are all present at once, scrambled together, just waiting for that little box to take them and sort them out? What do you take us for anyway—a bunch of gullible greenhorn fools?"

"And besides," continued an engineer, "how do these pictures get into the air in the first place? Where do they come from?"

"They're sent from a satellite in the sky," the traveler said, as all heads looked up. "You can't see it, of course. It's too high. But it's there."

"And of course you expect us to believe in something we can't see," said one of the scientists, with a touch of scorn.

"Believe it because of its effects—the results—the evidence of its existence," the traveler said. "If it weren't there, you would see no pictures."

"We know you're lying," another engineer said. "Even if there were a device in the sky, held up by a balloon or whatever, it couldn't send a signal down here without a wire. That would be against everything we know about electricity. And I don't see any wire."

"Well, it doesn't use a wire," said the traveler. "The signals are sent through the air. And the satellite isn't held up by a balloon; it stays up because it's high enough so that gravity doesn't pull it down."

"Now he's denying the law of gravity again," said one of the scientists. "Let's go. I've heard enough. Whatever he does to perform his little trick, he isn't telling us about it, so let's just leave."

"Yeah, let's get out of here," another scientist said. "Every time we catch him in an impossibility, he tells us the explanation is in the sky." Then turning to the traveler to say goodbye, he added, "We cannot believe something when the weight of scientific evidence is against it."

"But when the physical evidence is clearly before you," said the traveler, "how can you not believe, even if your theories cannot explain it?"

"Because such an event would be a miracle, and science has nothing to do with miracles."

"Then perhaps science is the poorer for it," said the traveler, sitting down to watch his television, which just then happened to be showing a dove flying silently across the sky.

✠✠✠

A FISH STORY

The bright sun and the gentle wind had made the little fish almost bold that summer day, enough so that they were swimming all over the pond, from their home in the reeds at one end to the rocky beach at the other. Or at least they swam very near to the rocky beach—as near as they dared—for all the older fish constantly warned them to stay away. Some of the dangers were clear enough, such as the wading birds who stepped into the shallow water, hoping to pluck out a little fish and swallow him right down, and the foxes, whose gigantic teeth were too awful even to think about. But there were other evils that were not so distinct. Hideous and unimaginable these were, with tales of fish swimming into the area and never to be heard from again, vague reports of sudden disappearances, and some hysterical tales, impossible to make sense of, of leaping shadows, wild splashings, worms flying through the water, and such like.

The dangers of the rocky beach could not quite be isolated in the minds of the little fish, so that they felt a general sense of impending doom whenever they swam more than a few feet from home. That is why, one day when three little fish met each other suddenly among the reeds, they were all momentarily startled. But soon they began talking and relaxed a little. "This is a wonderful pond," said one. "It's so big. But I've never been this far away from home before."

"Me either," said another. "I just hope we're safe here in these reeds."

"I do too," agreed the third. "You never know where

an enemy may come from."

"And you can't be too careful," added the first.

"By the way," said one, "my name is Swimmy Fish. What's yours?"

"Finny Fish," said another.

"I'm Chirpy Bird," said the third.

Swimmy Fish and Finny Fish gave a start, looked at each other with surprise and terror, and then swam off in opposite directions as fast as they could. "Wait!" cried Chirpy Bird. "What's wrong? Come back!" He looked around anxiously, himself frightened by their fright, though he could see no sign of danger anywhere. But their fear hung over the area, so he decided to swim toward home, at more than his usual speed.

He had not gone very far when he saw several adult fish swimming toward him with serious and half-frightened expressions on their faces. When they saw him, they stopped at a distance. "Stop there," one of them demanded, so Chirpy Bird stopped. The big fish seemed to be engaged in a solemn discussion. Every once in awhile one of them waved a fin or glanced in his direction. Finally, two of the largest fish approached a little nearer. "Don't make any sudden moves," the largest one, whose name was Glubber Fish, said with a mixture of command and pleading.

"I don't understand," the little fish said, bewildered.

"Are you Chirpy Bird?" asked Glubber Fish.

"Yes. I—"

"You must leave the pond." It was a tone of finality.

"But why?" asked Chirpy Bird.

"Because you'll soon be eating us and our children. Besides, birds don't live under water."

"But I'm not a bird," Chirpy Bird protested.

"What's your name?" demanded the other, who was called Spotted Fish.

"Chirpy Bird. But—"

"There you are," he said, with a tone of satisfaction.

"My name is Chirpy Bird," said the little one, "but I'm a fish."

"Nonsense," grumped Spotted Fish. "Whoever heard of a fish named Chirpy Bird?"

"Whether you've heard of me or not, here I am," said Chirpy Bird, not knowing what else to say.

"Totally illogical," interrupted Whisker Fish, who had just come near.

"As well as disrespectful and impudent," added Glubber fish.

"You must listen to reason," said Whisker Fish, self-importantly brushing himself in preparation. "And here it is: You are Chirpy Bird; granted. Birds eat fish; granted. Therefore, you eat fish."

"But—" Chirpy Bird tried to explain.

"There is no 'but.' It's a syllogism, and cannot be answered. The conclusion follows necessarily," said Whisker Fish. "It's pure logic."

"And it also follows," said Glubber fish, "that you must leave the pond."

"I'll die if I leave the pond," said Chirpy Bird.

"That's not our problem," said Glubber Fish.

"And it's an irrelevant objection," added Whisker Fish. The rest of the adult fish had gradually been easing forward during this conversation and now, at the direction of Glubber Fish, the whole group escorted Chirpy Bird down toward the rocky beach. In a few minutes they reached a low spot near a weeping willow, where several of the large fish grabbed Chirpy Bird and threw him onto the shore.

"Now fly away and leave us alone," one of them said. And leave them alone he did.

✠✠✠

MAN

Somewhere in a deep, tropical jungle lived a tribe of natives with extremely odd behavior. Generations ago the tribe had in some obscure fashion contracted a parasite which induced a seemingly permanent delirium in each native, and which was passed on to subsequent generations. The delirium increased with age, and most of the adult natives showed it by eating dirt, sleeping on dunghills, pummeling anthills with rocks even as the ants bit them severely, and jumping out of trees onto their heads. This last maneuver caused the natives to stagger around senseless for days, or simply to lie unconscious and bleeding in the sun and rain. All these symptoms together prevented the natives from caring for their personal lives, and so they lived in deplorable squalor, with their huts falling apart, and their children and themselves half starved and wholly naked.

Another odd effect of the mental distraction was an unnatural craving for firewood. Unlike the other natives in the area, the members of this tribe collected — and stole, and cheated and betrayed for — log upon stick to pile next to their huts, even though in twenty very cold years they couldn't use half as much as they already possessed. A few natives had been crushed to death by collapsing woodpiles; many more had died from fighting over decidedly unimpressive old branches.

One day a doctor came from the East to the village, and he immediately recognized the symptoms of the disease (a common one) for which he carried the cure. He went gladly and confidently to the chief of the tribe and announced his ability to remedy the ills of the people, expecting to be praised and welcomed for his offer of help. To his surprise, however, the chief rebuffed him with contempt and asserted boldly that there was nothing at all wrong with his people, that they had always acted that way since he could remember, that it was the human condition, and that they were all perfectly happy. Then, after ordering the doctor to leave immediately, the chief jumped out of a tree into the tribal latrine and was unavailable for any further discussion.

Substantially taken aback but firm in his resolution, the doctor decided to take his offer directly to the natives. Most received him with laughter, contempt, or violence; many ignored him; a few beat him up; some said he just wanted to get at their firewood; most said they, like the chief, felt fine. But a dozen or so natives came to him privately where he had been tossed into the bushes after his most recent beating, and asked him for the medicine.

"We are somehow not really happy living like this," they said, "even though it is the way of the world." The doctor gladly gave them the medicine, and in a few days they began to show remarkable signs of recovery. No longer desiring to eat dirt or jump out of trees, these natives corrected their diet, improved in health, and began to apply themselves to such activities as making baskets, repairing their huts, caring for their children, and gathering food. Some even began to question the wisdom of collecting stacks of wood more than twenty feet high.

Such wild, unusual, and anti-social behavior did not go unnoticed by the other natives, who quickly ostracized the cured natives from the tribal camp, calling them enemies of the current system. And even though many of the delirious natives began to suspect that the cured natives were somehow better off than they, and that there might be more to living than sleeping on dunghills and finding new trees to jump out of, resistance to the cure was strong. First, almost all the educated and respectable people — the chief and his council — spoke against it, and the example of their sophistication and wealth (the chief's woodpile was ninety feet high) was very strong. Many others, from the gossips to the wise man, said that the old way was right, and that the tribe had always behaved that way. There were few real individuals in the tribe, so that even though scores would have been glad to try the cure, they were afraid to stand against the rest and did what everyone else was doing, which was nothing.

The witch doctor had a stronger argument against the new regimen. He pointed out that the cure was harder to take than the cures he dispensed. The Eastern doctor's cure was painful, and though many of the witch doctor's cures caused vomiting, hives, convulsions, and hallucinations, the natives were all familiar with these effects and attributed them to swallowing the medicine wrong, rather than to the medicine itself. But who knew what the fate of the cured natives would eventually be?

The cured natives said they felt fine, but they might have been lying. And who was fool enough to trust an outsider, a stranger, rather than the familiar witch doctor, who cursed those who took the cure because they rejected his medicines as false and pernicious? The cured natives said that a commitment must be made to trust the Eastern doctor; this was too difficult or uncertain a step for many, especially in the face of the social pressure around them. A decision accompanied by fear, decried by the important, and rejected by society could not be made by everyone.

After the time of his stay was over, the Eastern doctor showed the cured natives how to compound the medicine and then left. As generations passed, most of the natives remained loyal to the dunghill, but a few took the cure.

✠✠✠

LOVE

Otto and his girlfriend Brissa were driving merrily down the middle of the road one rainy night on their way to a party when they approached a little old lady trying vainly to change a flat tire.

"Gee, that's too bad," said Brissa.

"Yeah," agreed Otto.

"Maybe we should help her," added Brissa.

"We? You mean me. I'm not going to get wet. Besides, what good would it do me to help her? I don't even know who she is, and she probably doesn't have any money, or at least not enough to make getting wet worthwhile."

"But it would make you feel good to do a good deed," Brissa offered.

"Well, it makes me feel good to stay in here and keep dry," snapped Otto.

"It would make me happy, Otto," said Brissa, in her softest, most feminine voice.

"You? Boy, you're awfully selfish. Always thinking about yourself. You know, I wasn't put here just to cater to your stupid, idle whims." As his anger rose, Otto sped up a little, just in time to hit a large puddle near the little old lady, drenching her in a sheet of muddy water.

"Stop, Otto!" Brissa cried, exasperated. "I'll help her."

"Aw shut up," Otto snarled. "Do you think I'm going to walk into the party with a girl who's all wet and disheveled, looking like a drowned rat? You want people to laugh at me? Think of somebody besides yourself for a change. Now fix your makeup and keep your mouth shut."

✠✠✠

INDECISION

Once upon a time a dozen or so curious travelers rented a boat for a cruise out to an enchanted island, where, it was said, Athena sat on her throne dispensing rich gifts to all. The trip was smooth enough for awhile, with only a few rough seas to endure and an occasional shoal to avoid. But then one morning one of the passengers discovered that the boat was taking on water.

"We're sinking, we're sinking!" some of the people cried.

"No," said the captain, "the flow is not yet so fast. If we will get some buckets and bail the water out, everything will be all right." This solution seemed simple enough.

However, a dissension soon arose among the travelers about who would do the bailing, and what buckets would be used. "Allow me," said one. "It is my duty in this circumstance to bail, and I have here a very solid bucket suitable to the task."

"Beg pardon, sir," said another, "but I must be the bailer. It is written in the laws of the sea that a person of my parts must do this labor. Besides, I have a superior bucket."

"Wait," said a third. "This gentleman's bucket is all right, but I think I should be allowed to help bail, since I am a fellow passenger."

Everyone adduced many weighty, true, and worthy philosophical arguments for his position, and cited laws, ethics, and political and procedural rules, but no person succeeded in convincing any other. Soon, therefore, the discussion ceased to remain at this level, but grew rather heated, and shouts and aspersions began to fill the air, with perhaps even a trace of ill will.

"I refuse to allow anyone to bail this boat unless he uses this bucket, which, as any fool can see, is the only true bucket, clearly superior to all others," screamed one.

"And I absolutely refuse to see this boat bailed unless I can take part in the work," yelled another.

Now these passengers all had some interest in seeing the boat bailed, and most hoped that this impasse could be overcome to the satisfaction of everyone. But since no one knew exactly what to do, nothing was done.

"Perhaps we will get to the enchanted island without bailing the boat," hoped one.

It was not to be so. While the travelers continued to debate, some suggesting unworkable alternatives and the others remaining unyielding, the boat continued to fill, until at one sudden and horrifying moment, the water rushed in over the gunwales and across the deck. The hold filled rapidly, and in spite of every man's frenzied efforts, the boat sank, carrying the stubborn but now too-late-repentant travelers, together with their screaming wives and virgin daughters, to the very bottom of the sea.

✠✠✠

THE LIMIT

One day a man was walking through a forest and got lost. "Nothing could be worse than this," he said. Then it got dark. "Lost in the dark. What could be worse?" he asked. Then it got cold. "Now nothing could possibly be worse," he said as he shivered and stumbled around But then it began to rain. "How could anything be worse than this?" he asked himself. But then the rain turned to snow and the wind came up. "This is absolutely the worst possible thing that could ever happen," he said. "There's nothing left." But then he fell and broke his arm. "Well, that's it," he thought. "This is the worst of all." But as he lay in the snow, a tree branch broke off and fell on him, breaking both his legs. "This is worse than the worst," he thought. "But at least nothing else can happen." But then he heard the sound of wolves coming his way. The noise was so startling that the man awoke and discovered that he had been dreaming. "What a dream I had," he said, shaking himself. "Nothing could be worse."

✠✠✠

HOW SIR REGINALD HELPED THE KING

Once upon a time in the kingdom of Plebnia, the king was having a real problem with his letters to the outlying regions. His messages always seemed to arrive too late. No matter how early he mailed them, his Christmas cards arrived in July and his Valentines arrived on December 24, creating confusion and uncertainty among the people and giving the Problem Element an excuse to arouse the Rabble against him.

After some thought, the king had an idea: he would give ten million greedos (their monetary unit) and the hand of his totally gorgeous daughter to the person who could make his mail arrive the fastest. His loyal subjects immediately rushed to solve the problem, setting themselves to this task with an enthusiasm that an objective observer might well have described as manic. People ran back and forth, up and down, muttering, "Move the mail, shove the mail, fling it, sling it. Run. Hurry. Shoot the mail, toss it, heave it," and such like.

Included in the many and varied offered solutions were proposals to build a rocket sled, crisscross the countryside with pneumatic tubes, use fast horses stimulated by strong coffee, borrow a dragster from the sports arena, set up a reliable airline, make a jet-powered conveyor belt, or just use ordinary mailmen under the threat of immediate, violent death if they delayed the mail.

However, Sir Reginald, the young, handsome hero of this tale, out of the goodness of his heart, his love for the king, and the excitement of the challenge (and scarcely considering the money or the girl more than four or five hours a day), decided to take a few minutes to examine the problem before he tried to solve it.

"Just what is it the king wants to do?" he asked himself. "He wants to send his mail quickly. And just what is mail? It's a message, information. Information, hmm. Information can be sent electronically, by wire or transmission. Yes. Hmm. Yes—A transmitter on one end and a printer on the other end would permit the king's mail to be sent at the speed of light. That should pretty much squash Sir Rodney's proposal to use battery-powered frisbees."

Well, what can we say? The brilliance of this proposal was so obvious that Sir Reginald was declared the winner and the plan was immediately instituted. The mail began to arrive on time, the king soon became popular again in the outlying regions, and Sir Reginald retired to spend the rest of his days in a spiffy castle on top of a hill, with his totally gorgeous wife and, later, seventeen children.

✠✠✠

HOW THE NOBLE PERCIVAL WON THE FAIR ARISSA

Once upon a time in a kingdom by the sea, two knights stood talking about the strategy of battle when their conversation was interrupted by the sight of the beautiful Arissa as she walked upon the green. "Forsooth, I think I'll ask her for a date," said Sir Wishful, one of the knights.

"Ditto," said Sir Percival, the other knight.

So Sir Wishful sauntered up to Arissa in his most elegant and refined manner, and, twirling his mustache genteelly, said, "Arissa, my dear, methinks I'd like to take you out to dinner."

Arissa sized up Sir Wishful a moment and then replied, "Sorry, Wishy, you're not my type."

Sir Percival, seeing his rival stumble off in a confused, embarrassed, humiliated, dazed—oh, you get the idea. Anyway, Sir Percival saw his opportunity and approached Arissa. "Arissa," he said, "how about a date anon?" Only a moment was needed for the look of mild surprise to alter the beautiful maiden's features, after which she laughed loudly in Sir Percival's face for a good ten minutes.

Well, both Sir Wishful and Sir Percival retired to lick their wounds and lament the fate of men in this whole romantic con game, and Sir Wishful soon enough decided that he liked the taste of trout just about as well as the taste of women's lips, so he grabbed his bait and tackle and headed for the river. Sir Percival, on the other hand, really thought Arissa might be worth another attempt, and he rationalized with himself that perhaps she didn't quite understand the question. "Or belikes the maiden is just shy," he thought.

So Sir Percival, seeing on another day the fair, delicate Arissa using her footman's coat to clean the mud off her shoes, again approached and asked: "Arissa, sweet one, won't you go out with me sometime?"

Arissa generously gave Sir Percival a look that could have frozen several pounds of choice lobster, and replied, "You must be kidding."

Sir Percival thought about this answer for a couple of days, and still finding his inclination toward the gentle Arissa unchanged, he thought to make a clarificatory attempt, just in case the maiden did believe he had been kidding. Approaching her the next morning, Sir Percival said, "Kind Arissa, I wasn't kidding the other day. Ifay, I'd like to date you."

Only the author's extreme commitment to complete truth forces him to admit that a tiny trace of irritation now flashed, but only for the briefest of moments, across the lovely Arissa's brow. "Get lost, creep," she said, clearly and distinctly.

Well, needless to say, by now most of the other knights in the realm were getting sufficient jollies out of Sir Percival's romantic endeavors. Even Sir Wishful had joined in the laughter, ridicule, and derision that seasoned Sir Percival's every meal with his friends. This hilarity touched the young knight and caused him to spend several days in contemplation of his past behavior. "Am I gaining or losing ground with Arissa?" he asked himself. "Rather had she said, 'Get lost' before she said, 'You must be kidding,' for as it stands, I can't say I'm making much progress."

But "Steadfast" was probably Sir Percival's middle name (or his uncle's middle name, anyway), so the knight decided to approach Arissa yet again. After all, Arissa seemed to be pretty okay, and Sir Percival wanted a date. In a few days, then, Arissa heard a familiar question in a familiar voice: "Arissa, sweetheart, let me ensconce you in my carriage and take you on a date."

To which Arissa replied, "Sorry Perce, I'm busy. I've got to wash my hair."

To which the knight: "Well, when could you go then?"

To which Arissa: "Well, I'll be busy for the next ten years. I mean, I've got stuff to do, forsooth."

Well, our hero was getting a bit despondent about all this, and for sure his friends weren't helping much. Far from their giving him encouragement, their laughter rang so constantly in Sir Percival's head that he began to wonder if he was still quite sane. And not a few of his friends hinted here and there that psychiatric consultation might be useful to the knight, to get him over his ridiculous interest in the agreeable Arissa.

About this time it so happened that as Sir Percival was on his way to visit Sir Wishful for a nice dinner of trout and onions, he quite unexpectedly came upon Arissa, lovely as ever, sitting near the village waterfall and picking her teeth. Almost out of habit, Sir Percival spoke: "Arissa, sugar, would you like to go out with me sometime?"

To which Arissa: "Oh, Perce, didn't I tell you I was busy?"

To which Sir Percival: "Yeah, fair one, but I thought maybe you'd had a cancellation or something."

To which Arissa: "Well, if I did have a cancellation, I wouldn't fill it up with you. Besides, what would we do?"

To which Sir Percival: "We could go to dinner."

To which Arissa: "Like where, ifay?"

To which Sir Percival: "Andre's French Victuals."

To which Arissa: "And when would this be?"

To which Sir Percival: "I dunno. How about tomorrow night?"

To which—well, anyway, to her own surprise, to the

astonishment of Sir Percival, and to the great confusion of the rest of the kingdom, Arissa finally actually agreed to this scenario and the next evening the two young people went to Andre's.

Arissa, of course, ordered the eleven most expensive things on the menu, for she was still intending to discourage Sir Percival, but the knight was willing to put up with only a glass of water for his own dinner, because the success he had enjoyed so far with the desirable Arissa had quite taken away his appetite anyway.

In the course of the evening, Arissa happened to remark, "I wish they had apricots on the menu here. You know, I really love them. I could eat them by the ton."

To which Sir Percival: "Why, Arissa, my dove, I own an orchard of apricot trees."

To which Arissa: "Really? Oh, Perce." When she pronounced his name, the young maiden sighed and a glisten appeared in one or both eyes.

Well, from here the story gets pretty mushy, so we'd better make it short. This delightful couple soon held hands; they discovered anon that their lips fit together pretty well, Arissa's ten years' worth of plans were miraculously cancelled, and Sir Percival finally asked the Big Question, to which Arissa replied, "Well, okay."

And so they were married and lived happily ever after, with Arissa often telling Sir Percival how she had secretly loved him from the first time she saw him, while Sir Percival, each time he kissed Arissa's apricot-flavored lips, congratulated himself for his skill in winning her.

✠✠✠

TRUTH CARVED IN STONE

A wise old philosopher was walking through the park with a young man and his true love when they came upon a beautiful statue of a Nereid. "Come here," he said to the youth, "and touch this statue." The young man put his hand on the statue's arm and felt of it closely, though he did not seem surprised at what he found. "Now the girl," the old man continued; so the lover also felt of his girlfriend's arm, in the same way. "And now," the man said, "tell me what you have learned."

"I'm not sure," the young man began. "The statue is hard and cold; the girl is warm and soft. Her flesh yields when I press; the marble does not."

"You have learned well," concluded the philosopher, "and if each of you remembers and lives by these truths, you will have a happy life together."

✠✠✠

How Sir Philo Married a Beautiful Princess Instead of the Woman He Loved

Once upon a time — and it had to be pretty long ago, as you will see — there lived a bunch of people in a little inland kingdom. The king, Cleon the Modest, was basically a good fellow, though he was not known for his brilliance in government. Instead, he was known chiefly for his glowing and nubile daughter, Jennifrella, a girl, though proud and a trifle petulant, so freighted with beauty and charms that pretty much every bachelor — and not a few married men — in the kingdom dreamed about her, whether awake or asleep. Truly, she maketh my pen tremble even as I write this.

Now Cleon was desirous of marrying off this legendary beauty as soon as possible so that he could be free of the constant entreaties for her hand, free of the frequent bills for supplying her dressing table, and free to spend more time in his rose garden, which he truly loved. The king would have had little trouble choosing the richest suitor in the kingdom for his daughter, except that there were no exceptionally wealthy bachelors in the realm, and those of modest wealth all had castles and money boxes of essentially similar dimensions.

For her part, the Princess Jennifrella was repletely enamored of Sir Fassade, a handsome, dashing, suave, carefree young knight who most people, when they faced reality, agreed would almost certainly become her husband and therefore the next king.

King Cleon, however, was desirous of exercising his regal authority in having a say in who would follow him on the throne. And faced with what he clearly saw was an impossible number of choices, he therefore sought the opinion of his favorite advisor, the young Sir Philo. Now, persons of a cynical bent might begin to think that Sir Philo, an eligible bachelor himself and not at all impervious to feminine gorgeousness, would argue craftily that he himself was the most suitable and worthy candidate. This might have been so but for two equally powerful reasons. First, Sir Philo, brave, skilled, and thoughtful, was a man of integrity who would never abuse his position as the king's advisor to advance his own interests, even in a matter so emotionally and biologically compelling as that before us. The other reason is that Sir Philo was already in love with another. It was a gentle love, like a deep river, quiet and calm on the surface but fully substantial and powerful in its flow.

His happiness, the Lady Lucinda, though not of outward visage the equal of Jennifrella, was handsome enough for the young knight's daydreams. When asked what attracted him to Lucinda, he would answer ambiguously or mutter something about the light in her eyes. What joy he got sitting with her under a tree in the bright spring, gazing upon her and dallying with her fingers or brushing a love-sick gnat from her collar. But what really twirled Sir Philo's cuff links was Lucinda's wit, her laugh, her playfulness. He relished taking the sprightly maid hand in hand on long walks, listening to the music of her voice and to the sentiments accompanying the music. How he loved to play with her tresses, or when her hair was up, to steal up behind her and kiss her unexpectedly on the back of the neck: for she would invariably produce a little shriek of surprise and delight and embarrassment, and then turning to him, her cheeks glowing irresistibly, attempt to glare and call him "monster," only to spoil her mock anger by bursting into giggles or even outright laughter. She would chide him and call him "rogue," and "impertinent," and he would say something like, "I'll put a stop to this abuse," and then their lips, who were old friends by now, would once again meet for fellowship. Of course, Lucinda would struggle just enough to enhance the enjoyment, until laughter or an unexpected visitor broke their embrace.

Well, enough mush. The point is that an unspoken understanding had developed between them so that only a few months after the rest of the kingdom knew it, they realized that they would one day wed and together laugh and cry through the years until death should wake them.

But to return to the weightier problem of King Cleon. Upon being asked for his advice, Sir Philo recommended that the king choose from among the following options. One, his majesty could choose the wisest and most just suitor for Jennifrella, for such a man would not only make a good king, but he would most likely be a decent husband, too. Or secondly, the king might seek a foreign alliance and marry his daughter to another king's son. This was an alternative which Sir Philo did not recommend, but mentioned only for the sake of completeness. And finally, the last possibility would be to let Jennifrella choose for herself—in which case, everyone knew that Sir Fassade would be the next king, and he, opined Sir Philo, would be "acceptable," producing a government no worse than the current one. (Since I have already described the king's advisor as "thoughtful," I shall now add "tactful" and note that the final participial phrase of the previous sentence was thought but not uttered by the knight.) As for the kind of husband Sir Fassade would make, the princess would have no one to blame but herself.

King Cleon thought the matter over not quite long enough and decided to hold an archery contest, the winner of which would marry his daughter. The degree of Sir

Philo's consternation is not recorded in the annals from which I am plagiarizing, but one may suppose that it was substantial, for reasons which will hereinafter appear. Needless to say (except to make the story longer and extend the reader's pleasure), Sir Philo made energetic protests, which eventually descended to rather pathetic entreaties, all in a futile attempt to change the king's mind. But King Cleon would not be dissuaded, and so the news was soon heralded throughout the kingdom, and, as you might suppose, arrow sales shot up immediately and remarkably.

As when a child pounds the ground near an anthill, causing a good many of the residents instantly to surface and run around in massed panic, so on the day of the contest the world arrived in a swarm at the castle of Cleon the Modest and prepared to be a witness, if not the victor, in the winning of Jennifrella.

There were several dozen contenders in the contest, some quite accomplished archers, some more or less dilettantish, and quite a few whose skills put the spectators at random hazard. Amid the noise and enthusiasm on this day stood a grim and silent Sir Philo, deeply troubled about the proceedings for three reasons. First, strictly from a philosophical standpoint, a shooting contest was a completely irrational method of choosing either a spouse or a future king, and irrationality like this always troubled the young knight.

Second, though Sir Fassade was a very good shot, capable of satisfactorily humiliating most of the other contestants, he was no match for Sir Bargle. If they used the word then, I would have to exaggerate only slightly to say that Sir Bargle was, as they say in French, or maybe don't, a *jerque*. He punctuated nearly every sentence with an oath or a belch, constantly leered at the ladies in waiting (who knew all too well to keep a safe distance from him), and those who attended carefully to his speech noted that the word he used more than any other was "me." In a word (or fourteen, actually), Sir Bargle was a man unlikely to put his personal appetites in second place. The prospect of this knight nuzzling the hair or nibbling the earlobes of Jennifrella was in itself sufficiently revulsive to Sir Philo; the prospect of his becoming king was absolutely unthinkable.

The third reason that the king's advisor was grieved about the "score ahead and wed" method of selecting the princess' groom was that the only person in all the realm who could outshoot Sir Bargle was — Sir Philo.

Prithee, talk not to me about psychic conflict — nay, psychic trauma, for I have seen it here, and it is not gentle. Sir Philo traced and retraced many steps around the castle grounds, without thought of direction or destination, the movement of his feet and the tension on his face reflecting the turmoil in his soul. At length, in his anxiety, the brave knight turned to his lady love for succor and advice, and she, with a swiftness that surprised him and a nobility that made him love her more deeply than ever, told him that of course he must put the interest of the kingdom above his personal happiness. She then flew into his arms and burst into inconsolable sobbing for longer than we have time to look in on.

The contest began and proceeded remarkably well, with only the loss of a too-curious cow and a few luckless birds at the hands of the less accomplished suitors. Sir Fassade shot well that day, achieving a personal best. As each arrow hit, closer and closer toward the middle of the target, it made the princess clap a little louder and leap with joy a little higher. A smirk of self-congratulation soon decorated Sir Fassade's handsome face.

A loud belch and a louder laugh announced the commencement of Sir Bargle's shooting. As predicted by Sir

Philo, Sir Bargle was an excellent shot. As each arrow landed a good handbreadth closer to the center of the target than any of those of Sir Fassade, the smiles on the faces of the princess and her favorite knight grew less and less until they had been completely replaced by somber looks on the knight and what might be described as silent hysteria on the face of the princess. The look on Sir Bargle's face at the conclusion of his shooting is a little too carnal for me to describe.

As he shot his set of arrows, Sir Philo was forced more than once, after he had fully drawn his bow, to pause, and to wait until a little tremble — attributed by the crowd to nervousness and eagerness to win Jennifrella — left his hands. As each arrow hit the target, remarkably near the middle, it also pierced the very center of Lucinda's heart. The young knight thought more than once about letting an arrow fly wide of the target, but he did his duty, though it brought grief to himself and devastation to the woman he treasured.

Sir Philo's smile as he took the hand of the princess was obviously forced, but no one noticed because Jennifrella was now bawling so spectacularly that the crowd, though not at all wishing to be unkind, found it, frankly, entertaining.

As it does for us all, time passed and life went on.

After a peculiar three years' delay, Lucinda finally made her choice from among several good offers and moved with her new husband to a remote part of the kingdom where it was reported that she was content, though some said that the cooler climate had somewhat subdued her well-known effervescence.

In the fullness of time, Sir Philo exchanged his sword for a crown and ascended the throne. He ruled wisely and justly, and the kingdom prospered. Hero that he was, he had mostly adjusted to the princess' personality, reminding himself as occasion required (and occasion did require), that not only had he acted for the good of the kingdom, but he had wed great beauty and, eventually, personal power. He further reminded himself that Jennifrella had made an adequate wife, even after her face wrinkled and her tummy pudged, and that she had proved to be a reasonable mother to his children. Whenever, in a moment of inattention, he discovered himself pining to enjoy a witty remark or some unguarded laughter, he quoted, hoping that it was true, the old proverb that "we grow most not when something is given but when something is taken away."

All in all, it was a reasonable life with much to be thankful for. Jennifrella's joy was that Sir Philo, now King Philo, remained a generous and loving husband even as her beauty faded; her only regret was that Sir Fassade had married her younger and more amiable sister, and both of them appeared to be altogether too happy. Lucinda's joy was in her two lovely children, whom she took, once or twice, to see the new king as he made a royal progress through their village. Her only regret was that she could reveal only half her heart as she told them what a good man he was. Sir Philo's joy was that he had acted virtuously and now enjoyed a mostly pleasant life, dispensing justice and mercy with care and humanity. His only regret was that he had learned to shoot arrows.

✠✠✠

SERENDIPITY

A young man, in the confusion and embarrassment of youth, was walking across the campus of a great university on the way to his philosophy class. At the previous meeting, the professor had posed the question, "If we do not know the purpose of something, how can we know whether any aspect of it is good or bad?" This question, together with the problem for the day, "Does man have a purpose?" had taken complete occupation of the young man's mind, not because of any intrinsic interest, but because the professor was in the habit of calling on students and expecting a thoughtful response. So deeply meditative was the young man that he neglected to observe his path adequately, with the result that he soon bounced his head off an unhappily placed tree in the middle of the lawn.

Picking himself up and dusting himself off, the young man looked around to see if anyone had witnessed his inadvertent folly. The only people nearby were two men, who, although they were just a dozen feet away, were completely oblivious to the young man's accident, for the reason that they were engaged in a somewhat heated argument. Whether to obtain some sympathy for his bruised head, or to excuse his inattention, or perhaps simply because they were standing near a wheel barrow and looked for all the world like gardeners, the young man interrupted them with the slightly exasperated question, "Excuse me, but what is that tree doing there, anyway?"

Now it so happens that these two men were not gardeners at all. They were, in fact, tenured professors of philosophy, the very subject the young man was struggling to understand. They turned to him at once and condescended to admit him to their conversation.

"Well," said the first philosopher, pushing his glasses up the bridge of his nose, "see here. This is a tree." And pointing to the tree the young man was already too-intimately familiar with, concluded with apparent satisfaction, "As Circumplexius has said in the fourth book of his *De Scientia*, 'An example is the best definition.'"

"I know that is a tree," replied the youth, rubbing his forehead. "What I want to know is, Why is it there in the first place?"

"You see," said the other philosopher to the first, "the dance of the blind with the senile." Then, momentarily stroking his beard, he turned to the young man and continued, "A tree means what it is. The concept of treedom does not subsist in some fortuitous, exogenous physical presence — that is the doctrine of carpenters, not of philosophers. As Herman of Rimboa has aptly remarked, 'Inner eyes must perceive beyond what the outer eyes see.'"

"And as the Chinese say, 'The flies buzz in the wind, but men drink their tea,'" added the one with glasses. "Here, son," he went on, pointing again, "this is also a tree. Compare them and deduce treehood by subtracting the anomalous from the universal."

"Certainly you have read Dohesius *On the Nature of the Universe* in the last twenty-five years," the other philosopher said with some indignation. "Don't you recall his dictum that 'a second example is not an explanation'? How do you pretend to instruct the ignorance of youth when you have never instructed yourself? 'The canvas remains blank when the artist has no paint,' says Hugo de Brassus. Go back to your books."

"And as de Roquefort says, 'To sit on a cheese and eat whey is the destiny of fools.'"

"See here, young man," said the beard, ignoring his colleague, "treeness is a life process displaying the aspiration of matter toward hierarchy, order, and structure. It finds analogues and even homologues in life systems everywhere."

"The frogs croak at night, but the sky remains dark," said the glasses, smirking slightly.

"Nonsense," replied the beard. "What I have said is self-evident. Sir Humphrey Boodle even noted it."

"But Boodle has been refuted these three hundred years."

"Well, Calesimon said so, too."

"Hah!" cried the glasses with a laugh of forced incredulity. "Calesimon! Calesimon was an idiot!"

"Argumentum ad hominem."

"Oh, come on. The man was institutionalized."

"And genetic fallacy, too. My, my."

"Ignore him, son," said the glasses to the youth. "He's not been very well since his wife laughed at his last paper. A tree —"

"She did not laugh," interrupted the beard.

" — is a woody plant containing specialized structures, larger overall than a bush and often, as you see here [pointing] having only one trunk rather than many."

"And is this the effect of dotage or of primordial ignorance?"

"False dilemma, Mr. Logician."

"Surely you were there that day in bonehead English when they distinguished between 'definition' and 'explanation.' You are familiar with the English language, aren't you? The young man has asked for an explanation."

"Well, as Frabonarde says, 'The whole is known by its parts.'"

"The doctrine of those who pull the wings from fruit flies."

"Yes, it would be too straightforward for someone who needs six hundred pages to discover that he doesn't know what he is talking about."

"A classic example of the projectionist error. Not everything you don't understand is a problem with the text," said the beard, tapping his finger to his temple.

"If I may be permitted one last allusion to Oriental wisdom, I would note only that the Chinese have said, 'Men hurt their eyes seeking a water lily in a rock garden — even in a large rock garden.'"

"I thought you knew that the Poems of Chen had been exposed as a product of nineteenth-century Europe. Don't make it a habit to go around quoting hoaxes. It gives philosophy a bad name."

"Excuse me, sirs," the youth interjected, "but I have to go now."

"Very well," said the beard. "Only remember, with the knowledge you attain, seek to achieve understanding."

"Oh, so now we are quoting the Bible!" cried the glasses with triumphant scorn. "The rest of the department will be interested in this."

"I was not quoting the Bible. I have never even read the Bible."

"Why don't you ask God to bless him while you're at it?"

"Listen, don't you think I know that your doctrine of cosmic mental states is just a front and that you're a closet monotheist?"

"And may I remind you that slander is an offense punishable by law?"

"And is this the state of a wise man?" asked the beard, looking at the sky, "to threaten his friend for speaking truth?"

"Now he's even praying! I can't believe this!"

"'We cannot see around corners,' says Germulphius,

'so what is left to the man who refuses to see in a straight line?'"

"Someone like your wife," answered the glasses. "No doubt by now she's found twelve more insupportably ridiculous assertions in your paper on aperceptual phenomenalism."

"Well, at least my wife reads my papers. At least my wife can read."

"My wife is an avid reader of literature."

"Since when did the television listings become 'literature'? That's the most transparent semantic ploy I have ever heard."

"Are you accusing me of owning a television?"

"He who can see the maggots need not ask if the dog is dead."

"'Ignore the shadow cast by a passing vapor,' says Phonetes."

"You've always been sloppy with bibliography, haven't you?" demanded the beard. "Phonetes would have been utterly embarrassed to have said that."

"No matter. Truth needs no ascription."

"That statement is obviously the product of extensive reading and protracted thought. With a little more effort, no doubt you'll be able to announce that the sun shines on a clear day."

"I suppose you have never read von Hoch: 'I had always known what he said, but I did not live it until I heard it spoken.'"

"I reject that statement together with its sordid implications. It smacks of the grimy hands of utilitarianism. In a minute you'll be insisting that philosophy have practical consequences for berry pickers and children. Perhaps you would be happier as some sort of mechanic where you could get your hands on things, rather than as one who pretends to instruct youth."

"You and Sir Peter Poole, who was proud that he couldn't tell a hoe from a rake."

"Well, what of that? My profession is philosophy, and I look for truth, not for mud."

"Even the sun cannot be seen through a silver coin."

"I have never accepted money for anything I've published," said the beard hotly.

"'Beware of those who look to the right and walk to the left,' says della Corta."

"How dare you accuse me—" At this point they were interrupted. A young man, deeply preoccupied with thinking about the purpose of mankind, had just bounced his head against a tree and—ah, but this is where you came in.

✠✠✠

A TALE REVEALING THE WISDOM OF BEING A CORK ON THE RIVER OF LIFE

Once upon a time, not very far from a town pretty much like yours, an old, nearsighted man was wandering down a country road quite pleasantly, musing to himself thusly: "I wonder what I should seek today? Some new treasure of the Orient, or a lost clue to the secrets of nature? That would be nice, as I spit" (and here, had there been but a small brass spittoon by the wayside, a clear ring would have sounded across the nearby pastures), "but," continued the old man, "this is pretty barren ground hereabouts, so I'd best not set my hopes too high. I'll start by looking for a silver dollar."

With this thought, the man's eyes brightened and he continued now more alertly down the road, staring intently at the ground and knocking little pebbles around with his cane. After a little, he thought he saw something ahead. Mending his pace somewhat, he hurried (as an old man with a cane hurries) up to the object, which he now believed to be a quarter. When he stooped down to pick it up, however, he found it to be merely a bottle cap, covered with red ants eating the remaining sugar. "Just what I was looking for!" exclaimed the old man with glee, even though the ants began to sting him on the thumb and forefinger. "Bottlecaps can be very useful." So he put the new possession into his pocket and once more began his stroll, still watching the ground.

He had hardly begun to wonder what he might find next, when, there, just a little way off, he saw a pearl lying in the roadbed. "Surely," he thought, "nothing is round or shiny exactly like a pearl, so I could not be mistaken this time." So he began to amble over without delay. As he came nearer, his joy increased. "Hee hee!" the old man laughed, before stifling his mirth lest he call attention to himself and bring competitors for his newfound treasure. He even paused a moment and looked around to see if anyone had noticed him or the pearl.

The way seemed clear so he closed the final distance, reached down, and picked it up. Instantly he was aware that this was no pearl, but just a partly dried up chicken brain, which must have fallen off some farmer's cart, or been left by some animal in haste. "Just what I was looking for!" the old man said very joyfully. "Chicken brains make real good soup." Into his pocket with the bottle cap went the brains, and down the road with his cane went the old man.

It was not long after this that he saw another, much larger item in the road before him, which looked, from where he now was, just exactly like a fat roll of paper money. Blessing his astrological reading promising riches for that day, he made his way up to the spot with a speed truly remarkable for a person of his age and infirmities, and anxiously bent over to retrieve his treasure. A closer look, however, and a confirming touch revealed that the man had found a "road apple," or, as it is sometimes called, a "horse biscuit." "Just what I was looking for," the old man said, now more perfectly pleased than ever; "I can use this biscuit to cook my chicken soup. Seems dry enough to burn right well."

Now the old man, between his nearsightedness and his preoccupation with his great discoveries, wandered unknowingly over to the side of the road, and pretty soon he stepped off into a ditch and fell down with remarkable violence. A farmer not very far off saw this episode, and hurried over to help the old man up. As he got to his feet, the old man, wincing with pain and holding one arm, cried out with a tone of satisfaction, "A broken arm! Just what I was looking for! A broken arm can be very useful." The farmer blinked once or twice, recognizing that this sentiment did not conform with what his own would have been under the like circumstances, but he said nothing. Instead, he quite generously helped the old gentleman into his cart and took him to town.

When the two arrived, the farmer dutifully summoned a doctor and the constable and some others of note in the place and repeated how the old man had fallen and broken his arm, only to exclaim that such a result was apparently what he had intended. This narrative caused some strange looks and a little discussion among them, and no one could think what to do next (aside from fixing the man's arm), when the constable suddenly remembered that he did not know the man's name. "Sir," he asked, "have you any identification?"

"Why, I think so, sonny," replied the old man, beginning to fumble in his various pockets, and then, to the indescribable surprise of his audience, to remove what they did not know, and could not have imagined, were the souvenirs from his previous wanderings. When his pockets were finally emptied, there was still no identification, but instead, on the table before them, his interrogators saw the following objects, namely, viz., and to wit: the bottle cap, the chicken brains, the horse manure, a piece of grimy string, a cigar butt, three pieces of chewed and flattened gum, a wing nut with stripped threads, a rusty nail (bent in two places), part of a candy wrapper, some rat pills (eleven of them), half a marble, and a common pebble.

After a moment or two of reflective silence, the mayor made bold to speak (seeing the constable in a reverie), and asked gently and softly, "Where did you get all these, uh, items?"

"Why, looking for gold and treasure, sonny," the old man answered, in a tone that implied that the mayor should have known the answer already. "But," he added as a second thought, and in the face of these gentlemen's now rather extravagantly and injudiciously raised eyebrows and opened mouths, "they were all just what I was looking for—like the broken arm here. Quite a find, eh?"

At this point, the farmer, who had been standing generally in the background holding his hat in both hands, came forward and begged an audience with the constable. "I didn't want to say this before," he began in a low tone, "but now I think I must, in case it should be important. All the way into town that old fellow kept saying something to me about wanting to cook his brains by burning a horse biscuit under his cap."

That was enough. And, needless to say, the Authorities from the Institution in the city were immediately summoned, and the old man was taken to a very pleasant place where he could rest among friends and nice people, have no worries, and be free to enjoy the "butterflies, blue skies, and happiness always." It is reported by reliable sources that shortly after arriving the old man was heard to exclaim cheerfully, "Just what I was looking for! Mattresses on the walls!"

✠✠✠

The Art of Truth

Once upon a time a famous art museum searched the world over for the best paintings it could find. After a long search, the museum found a beautiful Old Master painting depicting youths and maidens frolicking in a wood. The directors were only too glad to pay millions for this painting because they were captivated by its beauty and elegance. How delightfully the maidens' hair and mouths were drawn, how perfectly the hands and arms of the youths, how life-like the bare feet on the forest floor. But the curator of the museum was the happiest one of all, for he had now become guardian and protector of a famous work by a famous painter. "Every time I look at that painting," he would say, "I see new beauties and excellences. Just look at these leaves here, the sweep of the branches from this tree, capturing just the hint of a breeze and seeming to vibrate with the music from the dance of the youths and maidens in the clearing. My very soul resonates with the greatness of it all."

Needless to say, this wonderful painting was the most popular exhibit at the museum, providing instruction and delight for thousands of visitors. Everyone, from the young child who could barely walk to the old man who could barely walk, enjoyed its beauty frankly and openly or profited from studying its color and arrangement. Children loved to see the happy figures kicking up their feet with joy; the young people marveled at the freshness and beauty of the figures; those of mature years stood astonished at the excellent technique that could present such a convincing vision; the old remarked upon the feeling of cozy intimacy produced by the scene of innocent pleasure.

"This painting is almost too good to be true," remarked one visitor prophetically as he purchased a print of it.

One day a horrible discovery was made: the painting was not a genuine Old Master after all. It was a forgery. It had not been painted by the famous artist whose name was on it, and in fact it had been painted within the last ten years. The museum directors and the curator were horrified and consumed with shame. Immediately the painting was jerked from the walls of the museum and ignominiously relegated to a basement storeroom. "We regret such an unfortunate imposition," the curator told the museum's patrons. "This painting is not art; it is a tawdry fake. This painting is a lie."

At first the public was saddened to lose sight of such a popular painting, and a few mild protests were raised, but eventually concern for the painting was pushed aside by other more pressing concerns, and it was forgotten (as are all things no longer directly in front of us in this busy world) and life continued.

Only the museum curator and an occasional junior staff member ever saw the painting now, hanging in the dim light of the basement well away from public view. All that was heard of it was the curator's occasional disparaging comment. "Every day I see new defects and ugliness in this fraudulent outrage," he would say. "Just look how false the sun on the leaves looks, how phony is the wisp of that girl's hair, how ugly the clouds there, and how awkward that boy's position in the dance. How we were ever taken in by this obvious cheat is beyond me." And finally, shaking his head to show his regret, he concluded, "What we did was foolish and shameful."

✠✠✠

Matthew 18:3

"The door to this classroom is farther down the hall, sir," said the student.

"How dare you try to tell me where the door is," huffed the professor, as he turned around and walked abruptly into the wall. While he held his bleeding nose, he was heard to mutter, "Now why did they move the door?"

⌘ *A proud man never doubts, even when his nose bleeds.*[1]

✠✠✠

---

[1] "Truly I say to you, unless you are converted and become like children, you shall not enter the kingdom of heaven." — Matthew 18:3

THE BOY AND THE VULTURE[2]

A young boy was playing in the desert with a bow and arrow he had made, when a vulture, always looking for a tender meal, saw him from afar. The bird flew over and, seeing that the arrow was only a barren stick, swooped down and pecked at the boy. "Why don't you shoot me if you don't like my pecking?" it taunted. The boy shot his arrow repeatedly, but the bird was too quick, and the arrow always missed.

Finally, exhausted from chasing the arrow and deflecting the bird, the boy sat down in the sparse shade of a dead tree. The vulture, lighting on one of the dry branches above the boy, sat triumphantly preening and smirking, and even plucked a few old feathers to drop on the boy's head in contempt. "There's for your pains, feeble one," the bird said haughtily.

The boy, however, would not be defeated. Carefully he collected the feathers, fixed them to his stick, and with the resultantly accurate arrow, shot the surprised vulture through the heart.

⌘ *In our pride we often unwittingly give our enemies the means to destroy us.*

⌘ *Perseverance and ingenuity, even in the face of humiliation and defeat, will at last succeed.*

✠✠✠

---

[2] Suggested by Aesop, "The Eagle and Arrow."

Three Flat Tires

Once in the fullness and complexity of human existence three cars left the same party one rainy night and took three different roads on the way home. Oddly enough, at approximately the same time, each car suffered a flat tire, and the young couples inside suddenly found their evening and their lives somewhat different from what they had been expecting.

The young lady riding in the first car became instantly upset. "Well, this is just great," she said to her escort with understandable disgust. "I knew I should have driven; then this never would have happened. How could you be so careless when we're all dressed up like this, anyway?"

"I'm sorry," the young man replied, getting out of the car. "I'll fix it as fast as I can." He quickly retrieved the jack and the spare tire and began to puzzle over the repair. In a minute the young lady was at his side.

"You don't even know what you're doing, do you?" she asked.

"Well, not really, but I think I can figure it out," he told her honestly.

"No you won't. I want this done right," the young lady answered, as she grabbed the jack handle with just enough suddenness that the young man lost his balance and fell over backward into a patiently waiting mud hole.

While these events came into being to form a permanent, though small, part of the history of the universe, the young driver of the second car was, not many miles away, even then climbing out of his vehicle into the rain and opening the trunk. His date, in a very ladylike manner, and with due concern for her precious gown, stayed in the car with her hands folded in her lap. She generously took care to look away from the young man's labors in order not to cause him embarrassment, and, when he slipped down and bumped his head on the fender as he tried to loosen a particularly intransigent lug nut, she very kindly turned on the radio.

The third young man, though he encountered different raindrops on a different road on this night, realized similarly that he, too, was destined to be wet, and pushed open the door with resolve. However, as he climbed out of the car, the young lady he had been driving home got out also. "Get back in the car," he told her, "or you'll get wet."

"I'll help," the young lady said.

"There's nothing you can do," replied the young man as he reached for the spare in the trunk. "It's really a job for one person, and I've done it before."

"Then I'll watch," replied the young lady. And watch she did. Oh, she held the lug nuts to keep them from getting lost, but to speak truly, she was not really of any help and she did get drenched. As he changed the tire, the young man looked at the young lady once or twice, only to see her gown melting and her hair dripping down her face, and no doubt he thought, "What a sight she is."

Well, I've told you this story as evidence of the foolishness and irrationality of the human heart. For now observe the consequent:

The first young lady, naturally concerned for her safety and realizing that she possessed knowledge that her young man did not, quite reasonably chose to change the tire. However, the young man, fool that he was, was never seen escorting this capable and logical young lady again.

The second young lady, very sensibly concerned about preserving an expensive dress and realizing that she would be of little or no help to her young man, showed a similar wisdom in avoiding what she knew would be the consequences of leaving the car. But, even though her judgment was vindicated when she observed, in the form of the drenched, muddy, and bleeding young man, exactly those consequences she had predicted, the young man himself, blind and irrational as he was, was also never again seen escorting this thoughtful and discerning young lady.

Even stranger and more perverse as it must seem, however, the third young man, even after observing the silly and unreasonable behavior of his date, even after seeing her soaked to the skin, her gown ruined, her hair plastered against her neck, her mascara running down her cheeks in little inky rivulets—even after observing all this, not only was he seen escorting her frequently to other entertainments, but eventually he offered her a ring.

✠✠✠

THE HISTORY OF PROFESSOR DE LAIX

The world had long been promised a fifty-volume definitive analysis on the meaning of life by the brilliant and internationally respected Professor de Laix. Admirers from all across the surface of the earth produced unremitting and enthusiastic requests—nay, demands—for the wise professor to bestow upon the world his penetrating insights into human nature. As the years passed, however, even though he had been begged repeatedly for the first part, or a first volume, or even a first chapter, he had always answered that he wanted to get the whole work clearly in his head before he put it down on paper.

"To rush precipitously forward without knowing precisely where one wants to go," he would tell them, "will not of necessity produce a happy outcome because it might lead to a complicative erroneity or put one on a train to a destination he would not ultimately wish to visit. After all, the most beautiful part of a given day is known only after dark, and the best path up the mountain—which I take to be the path of true wisdom—is seen only from the top."

Year after year, therefore, arrived with hope and left disappointed; new generations were born and millions of hopeful readers mingled their own dust with that of the earth without the benefit of even a phrase of Professor de Laix' wisdom.

Then one spring his colleagues and students noticed that he was gradually becoming more and more animated, and was heard occasionally to mutter, "Yes, yes, that's right, that's right." Finally one day while he was sitting in a coffee shop regaling a few favorite students with tales of fruitless thinking journeys upon which he had in the past embarked, he took a sip of coffee (or perhaps he had inadvertently been served espresso) and then suddenly opened his eyes widely, sprang to his feet, and announced excitedly, "That's it! I see it all now! Now it can be written! Everything is completely clear! So clear! Ha ha! Now I understand! Now, at last, I understand!"

After this brief speech, he burst out of the coffee shop (leaving his students with expressions of amazement and an unpaid bill) and began to run toward his office where he could finally sit down and produce his great work. Now at last he could pour forth his hitherto inexpressible wisdom to fertilize the orchards of culture and bring into being a new and wonderful fruit for civilization to munch upon.

Unfortunately, in his highly focused and externally oblivious rush toward his office, he neglected to watch for the traffic as he crossed the busy boulevard between the coffee shop and the university (for academia is often separated from the rest of life by just such a metaphor), and as a result he was tragically but thoroughly run down by a fully loaded manure truck, whose cargo had been produced after only one day's rumination, and whose owner also hoped that it would swell the fruit on the trees of a less figurative orchard.

Such was the life and death of the great Professor de Laix, a man for whom someday almost came.

✠✠✠

HOW THE HUMANS FINALLY LEARNED TO LIKE THEMSELVES

It is man's peculiar distinction to love even those who err.
— Marcus Aurelius, VII.22
A sweet disorder in the dress.
— Robert Herrick

O nce upon a time, many years from now, technology had continued its remarkable progress to the point that the construction of artificial people had finally become possible. These humakins, as they were called, were made so carefully and with such art that no one could tell the difference between a real human and an artificial one—except that the artificial ones were flawless. Physically the humakins were always young, always beautiful, always fresh; they never had a hair out of place, never a pimple, never a wrinkle, never a gray hair. Mentally they were always bright, alert, and smiling; they always got their facts right, and never took a wrong turn or got lost.

At first the appeal of the humakins was irresistible, and most humans chose them over other humans for spouses. What human female could compete with an always slim, beautiful, and lively imitation? And what human male could compete with an always confident, correct, and handsome construction? In fact, the word "humakin" quickly became a synonym for "perfect," as in, "That's a really humakin car," or "This pie tastes just humakin." At the same time the word "human" became a term of opprobrium, indicating something defective or of low quality, as in, "I never shop there because it's such a human store with human-quality merchandise."

To the consternation of many, however, while the humakins could construct more of themselves in a factory, the humans could produce more of themselves only by following the ancient method of their ancestors, so that the result of the marriages between flesh and plastic was the eventual decline of the human race.

When about nine tenths of the persons on the planet consisted of the precisely fabricated humakins and only one tenth of the really human, quite an odd and unexpected situation arose. It had become so unusual to see, for example, a woman wearing glasses or a man with wind-blown hair that such a detail now took on a natural appeal to some of the other humans.

One bright morning at breakfast in a fancy resort dining room, a human female, almost as lovely as a humakin, sat chatting with a humakin male who had condescended to sit with her. Suddenly she inadvertently spilled a glass of tomato juice onto her white tennis dress. While her humakin companion predictably stood up and stared at her with horror, across the room a human male who had just witnessed the event was so filled with ardor and longing that he almost broke the table in his rush to get over to her and make her acquaintance. His excitement to declare his affection left him without the capacity for coherent speech, so that only tentative and confused phrases stumbled from his mouth. In the midst of his babbling, though, he could see, in the welling dew of the woman's eyes, the tenderness of regard he had inspired.

As other humans, too, began to grow weary of the expectation of constant perfection in their relationships, scenes similar to this one began to be repeated with increasing frequency. A loose shoe lace, a chipped fingernail, a shiny nose—all gradually became sources of romantic and emotional attraction, and those very characteristics that had before been viewed as defects soon came to be seen as emblems of the truly and desirably human, as guarantees of that unique inner fire that no amount of perfectly crafted plastic could equal.

The word "human" now began to be associated with the genuine, the natural — and the beautiful. It became not uncommon to hear a young lady remark to her admirer as he gently put a flower in her hair, "Oh, what a human thing of you to do." The word "humakin," on the other hand, began to imply something slickly unrealistic or laughably fake and was often pronounced with a sneer.

At length, having rediscovered the amorous appeal of their distinctives like freckles and missing buttons and the inability to refold road maps, the humans began to marry each other again. It wasn't many years before a young pledge of one of these new relationships was heard to ask in a tone of frustration, "But Mommy, why must I have a crooked tooth?"

To which the mother replied, "That's so I'll always remember how truly beautiful you really are."

᙭᙭᙭

THE CATERPILLAR AND THE BEE

A bee, flying proudly around the garden, approached a caterpillar sitting on a shrub. "I don't know how you can stand to be alive," the bee said. "I'm valuable to the world with my honey and wax, I can fly anywhere I want, and I'm beautiful to behold. But you're just an ugly worm, not good for anything. While I soar from bloom to bloom feasting on nectar, all you can do is creep around and chew on a stem."

"What you say may be true," replied the caterpillar, "but my Maker must have put me here for some purpose, so I trust him for my future."

"You have no future," said the bee. "You'll be crawling through the dirt for the rest of your life. If you ask me, you'd be better off choking on a leaf."

Sometime later the flowers in the garden woke to find that the bee and the caterpillar had both disappeared. All that they could see now was a shriveled yellow body hanging from the edge of a spider web and a magnificent butterfly flexing its wings in the sun.

⌘ *This story reminds us that we cannot predict the future, either for others or for ourselves.*

⌘ *This story teaches us to trust in God rather than in the opinion of men.*

✠✠✠

THE WISE ONE

High in the mountains of a distant land there once lived a man so incredibly old that his life no longer had any plot. He was so old that his very name had faded from the memories of all those around him, and he was knowr only as "The Wise One." He spent his later days hearing and commenting on people's problems and sitting among a dozen or two disciples who waited patiently to hear all that was asked of him and all that he spoke. Sometimes an entire day would pass when not a syllable opened his lips; whether this was from a temporary lack of strength or simply because he had nothing to say, no one knew.

While his reputation among his disciples and a few others was that he possessed amazing wisdom and insight, many people thought him to be an idle and incoherent fool because, they said, he never provided a practical solution to the problem he was asked about. Instead he would ask a simplistic question or tell a story whose point was so obscure that many left his presence shaking their heads.

Some said that in his youth he had earned and spent large quantities of money, only to turn from what he saw as a life of vanity to the pursuit of wisdom. Others said that had that been true, he was proved all the more fool for giving up the good life for a life of hardship that was of little use to anyone. Thus, for every person who called him The Wise One with reverence, twenty pronounced his name with irony.

Of the stories still not erased by the hand of time, consider these and judge the man as you will:

⌘ ⌘ ⌘

One day a man, clearly troubled by the cares of life, came to The Wise One and spoke thusly:

"My son, to whom I had entrusted my farm, last week stole my best cows, sold them in the market, and spent the money in wild and shameful living. Now he says he is sorry and will repay me. What should I do?"

"Tell me," replied the old man, "when you drop your bar of soap while bathing, what do you do?"

"I pick it up, of course," the man answered, with some irritation.

"And now tell me, which is of more value, a bar of soap or a human soul?"

While the questioner left not at all certain about what to do, one of The Wise One's disciples, who had been deeply affected by this exchange, rose and said, "Excuse me, O Wise One, but I must go and reconcile myself to a man I have wrongly ceased to love."

"Yes, my daughter," is all The Wise One said.

⌘ ⌘ ⌘

Another time a young couple came to The Wise One to settle a great argument. The old man listened seemingly more politely than attentively as each gave a lengthy explanation of the dispute. Finally the two looked to The Wise One for his decision, both of them more confident than ever of being right. The Wise One reached over to a vase sitting nearby and pulled out a rose. "Shall I hit you with the bloom or with the stem?" he asked the couple.

"And just what does that have to do with anything?" asked the young woman.

"It is written in the *Book of Worn Out Sayings* that 'in the rose garden of life he who plucks thorns for his partner's bed is a fool.'"

"I don't understand," said the young man.

"Those who sell flowers put them in a pan of colored water and the flowers take on the color of the water," concluded The Wise One. The couple left confused and without resolving their dispute, but they did seem to agree that their trip to The Wise One was worthless.

⌘ ⌘ ⌘

On one occasion two men came to The Wise One on the same day. The first was a young man unsure about which road to take as he stepped out into the world. "I have considered my career choices," he said, "and I don't know whether to become a poet or a merchant."

The second man had just married a wife and was about to buy a house for them to live in. "I have investigated many houses carefully," he said, "and have found two that would be suitable. The first house is nearly new and well designed but damp inside, while the second is light and airy but older and not so well designed. I don't know which to choose."

"Your problems are one," said The Wise One, as he picked up a honey comb and squeezed it until the honey was drained out into a bowl. "You both must choose between the wax and the honey."

"My gosh," said one of The Wise One's disciples, leaping to his feet, "I'm about to marry the wrong girl." And with that, he ran off into the distance.

The two men looked at each other, searching each other's face for a glimmer of understanding, which neither found.

⌘ ⌘ ⌘

One spring a richly dressed young man came to The Wise One and spoke these words:

"I have come from a far kingdom where I have just ascended the throne. My father ruled long and was old when he died, and now I am remodeling his castle. The many books of his great library are in the way of my new banquet hall, and I desire to rid myself of so much old paper. But I do not wish to throw out every book. I want to keep some for the sake of his precious memory. Thus, I have come to you for a principle of selection. Which books should I keep and which should I burn?"

"Go to the ancient source of rock in your kingdom, from which your cities have been built," answered The Wise One, "and build a pile of stones until you can stand on it and see over the edge of the quarry. Then remove the contemptible stones."

With a look of deep thoughtfulness on his brow, the young ruler left the presence of The Wise One and returned to his kingdom. It is not recorded whether this advice was put into effect or whether it helped the young ruler with his decision.

⌘ ⌘ ⌘

There are many other stories about The Wise One, just as there are many other people with their own stories. But these shall suffice to show how one old man exhausted the meager remnant of his days on earth. Whether his life was spent well or ill perhaps even he himself did not know.

✠✠✠

ON THE HEROIC SUFFERING OF MANKIND

A man stood philosophically on the prow of his ship, deeply inhaling the fresh sea air, feeling the warmth of the bright sunshine on his face, and ignoring or perhaps not hearing the burst of the whip as it lacerated the backs of the struggling slaves in the galley. But in the midst of enjoying his view, he felt a particle of dust fly into his eye. By blinking and rubbing it a little, he removed the speck, but his eye was reddened.

"Well," he said stoically, "life has many pains and hardships and we must bear them as best we can." Then relaxing upon a couch and ordering two slaves to dab his brow with a moistened cloth, he called upon his friends to sympathize with his suffering, whereupon he found some satisfaction in complaining of his hurt.

✠✠✠

THE QUEST

All literature is but a variation on the quest motif.
— Someone or Other
Too busy to look, too busy to be wise.
— Someone Else or Someone Other

There once was a man who wandered from town to town constantly examining the ground. He carried a lantern in the daytime and a compass at night. When asked what he was doing, he would answer, "I'm looking for a place to stand, so that when the wind blows I may stand and not fall."

Most people thought he was insane until a man who had lived long and experienced much was overheard to say of him, "Only a few people are as wise as this man, for he is engaged in the only search that really matters."

✠✠✠

LIFE

One day a man called his friend and invited him to lunch at his office. "Just come on over and we'll have a great time," the man said.

"Where is your office?" the friend asked.

"I'm not sure of the address," answered the man, "but it's somewhere downtown, I think."

"Well," asked the friend, "what does the building look like?"

"It's tall, like an office building."

"What floor are you on?"

"I think it's one of the middle ones."

"How many doors down from the elevator?"

"Oh, it's several. But I've never really counted them."

"Don't wait for me," said the friend, as he hung up.

⌘ *This is not a story about a man who could not give directions to his office. This is a story about the architecture of life. For many people inhabit their own lives in just this way, not knowing where they are or how to tell others how to reach them.*

✠✠✠

DISCERNMENT

B ut compared to the pearls, this piece of string is worthless," said the man, as he pulled it from the necklace and lost his whole treasure.

✠✠✠

IT DEPENDS ON HOW YOU LOOK AT IT: EIGHT VIGNETTES ON PERSPECTIVE

A man's house burned to the ground. Upon hearing of it, the man said angrily, "This is the fault of oxygen!" For, as he explained, if there hadn't been any oxygen in the atmosphere, his house never would have burned.

⌘ ⌘ ⌘

When the boss called Smervits and Jenkins into the office, Jenkins was very nervous because his plan to salvage the Freeble contract had not worked. Smervits wasn't worried because he had shrewdly stood by while Jenkins floundered with the contract.

"Jenkins, you failed," the boss said forcefully after the two men had entered. "That's good," he added, "because it shows that you tried something. Smervits, you didn't fail, but you didn't try anything. either. You're fired."

⌘ ⌘ ⌘

One day the power went off in the mine, leaving the miners in absolute darkness. One miner found a match and lit it. "What a dinky little flame," said one of his companions, with contempt.

"What a great light in the darkness," said another, with awe.

⌘ ⌘ ⌘

Just think," said the man in the orange hard hat, "to us that's just a useless pile of rock. But to someone with greater vision it has value. It can be changed by his direction into something useful."

"How's that?" someone asked.

"First it has to be crushed, and then heated in a furnace, to give up its old properties and take on new ones. Then it can be mixed with water and molded into something beautiful."

"So that's how you make cement, huh?"

"No," someone said, "that's how you make a Christian."

⌘ ⌘ ⌘

An officer came upon a young soldier so weighted down with weapons and ammunition that he couldn't move. "You know why you aren't attacking the enemy, don't you?" asked the officer.

"Yes," replied the soldier. "I'm waiting for more ammunition."

⌘ ⌘ ⌘

Once in a pleasant garden there stood a tree, from which, legend said, God himself would one day reign. But instead, a group of wicked men broke in and chopped the tree down. They hacked the tree into a beam and nailed a holy man to it, leaving him to die upon a hill. So the tree of hope now had become a beam covered with blood and death. "See here," the wicked men said, laughing with scorn, "in what manner God's promises are fulfilled."

⌘ ⌘ ⌘

The chairman of the department asked the young professor how his book was coming along. Said the professor, "Oh, the book is already written; I just haven't put it down on paper yet." The chairman patted the man on the back and told him to keep up the good work.

A construction worker, watching this scene transpire, decided that what was good enough for academe was good enough for him, so he sat back and opened a beer. Presently his foreman came along and wanted to know what was going on. Said the worker, "Oh, the hole is already dug; I just haven't taken out the dirt yet." The foreman, not having been enlightened by Higher Education, fired the worker, right in the middle of his beer.

⌘ ⌘ ⌘

A man on foot approached an abandoned auto wrecking yard that still had many old pieces of assorted cars lying around. "What an enormous pile of worthless junk," he said to himself as he walked by. The next day another man on foot approached the same yard. "What a wonderful pile of worthy raw materials," he thought as he surveyed the area. A few days later the second man drove away in his own car.

✠✠✠

The Strange Adventure

Once upon a time, so long ago that it seems like yesterday, circumstances so occurred that two youths found themselves lost together in the desert and forced to spend the night without the services of modern technology.

"What a terrible thing," said the first one. "We're stuck out here all alone among who knows what frightening stuff."

"This is great," said the other. "What an adventure. I can't wait to see what happens."

As the light began to fade, the youths happened upon a snake, sitting on a rock to get the last warmth it could find before the cold night set in.

"Oh, no!" said the first youth. "Out here it's just one problem after another. Now we'll have to worry about that snake crawling all over us as we sleep."

"What a great opportunity," said the second youth. "Now we can have some dinner." Soon the snake was roasting on an impromptu fire, and in a little while, the two youths began to eat.

"This is horrible," said the first youth, spitting out the meat and nearly vomiting. "I can't imagine a worse thing."

"Actually, it tastes rather mild," said the second youth, eating with relish.

When the next day came and the youths were rescued, they were asked about their adventure.

"It was the most awful, horrible experience I've ever had," said the first youth, trembling from the memory. "I'll be mentally scarred by it for the rest of my life."

"It was great!" said the second youth. "I think it's the best thing that ever happened to me. What a fun time. I'm so glad I was there."

⌘ *The events we experience are less important than the meaning we give to them, for life is about meaning, not experience.*

✠✠✠

IN DEFEAT THERE IS VICTORY

Once upon a time, among the infinite events which pass daily in this world, a man took his son and daughter to the racetrack to watch the horses run. After several races, the man announced that he would place a bet. "We want to play, too!" his children cried excitedly.

"Very well," answered the man. "Here are the names of the horses in the coming race: 1. Dotty's Trotter; 2. Sure Win; 3. Also Ran; 4. High Risk; 5. Looking Good; 6. Outside Chance; 7. King Alphonso."

"I want to bet on Sure Win," the boy said eagerly. "There's nothing like the certainty of success."

"And I will bet on Looking Good; he sounds so handsome and strong," the daughter said, with a trace of a sigh.

"Good, children," their father replied, and he went off to place the bets for them.

"Whom did you bet on, daddy?" the daughter asked when he returned.

"I bet on Outside Chance," he answered.

Soon the race started. The horses bolted from the gate and took off at top speed. Looking Good looked good around the first turn. "Yay, yay, yay!" the girl yelled, jumping up and down as the desire of her heart moved forward. "I'm winning! I'm winning!"

"Patience, my child," said her father. "In horse racing, unlike in life, we look only at the finish, not at the progress."

"I sure hope that's true," the boy said, "because Sure Win is running fifth."

"Yes, my son," replied his father, trying to soften an inevitable blow, "although you know you cannot gamble and be sure at the same time."

At length the horses came into the final stretch, and, except for King Alphonso, who trailed rather substantially, there were only a few lengths between the leader and the trailing horse. But in that final, all-consuming, frenzied gallop, where mere wish and common effort give way to inner strength and spiritual power, the spaces increased, so that finally the children, with their feelings crushed by the surprise of unexpected failure and by the dismay of dashed hope, watched the horses run across the finish line in this order: 1. Outside Chance; 2. Also Ran; 3. Dotty's Trotter; 4. Sure Win; 5. High Risk; 6. Looking Good; 7. King Alphonso.

While the girl burst into unrestrained sobbing, the boy, feeling the full difficulty of the conflict between youth and manhood, choked his tears back, and knowing his father to be a philosophical type, tried to see the metaphorical application of this event. "This race is an allegory, isn't it, Father?" he asked, "where we learn that to succeed we must avoid what appears to be a 'Sure Win' and apply ourselves instead to the 'Outside Chance.'"

"No, my boy," the man answered. "The lesson is that we should not pay attention to names and appearances, but that we should penetrate beneath the surfaces of things; that we must consider real abilities, evaluate past records, and trust our judgment to bring us to a knowledge of the truth. Appearances and labels are often false and seldom accurately reflect inner realities. We must not let our casual perceptions influence our beliefs or rule our actions. I bet on Outside Chance because he previously has consistently outperformed the other horses in today's race, or horses that have beat the others. I care not about his name. Read where it says that God does not judge by external appearances, and imitate him."

"But I still like Looking Good and I wanted him to win," his daughter said perversely, wiping her tears and stamping her foot. "Outside Chance is a creep."

"And now, my daughter," said the man, "you have first felt the conflict between reason and passion. May you learn to resolve it well."

✠✠✠

THE OPPRESSED GIRL

This may seem like a tall story, but there was once a teenage girl who didn't get along with her parents. "I'm sick and tired of all these oppressive rules," she would complain. "I feel just totally controlled. I want to be free!" So she ran away from home. "Now," she thought, "I can stay up all night and listen to loud music and watch awful movies."

When she told her friends of her new freedom, they said, "Great! Let's celebrate and get drunk."

"Yeah, why not?" she replied. "I can do anything I want." So she drank and laughed and vomited and passed out on the bathroom floor.

A little while later, she met an older girl who seemed to be experienced in the ways of freedom. "Hey," said the older girl, "to be free, just take these pills and free your mind from all your cares." So the teenage girl took the pills and felt strange and didn't sleep for three days and then closed her eyes and woke up in the middle of the following week.

Another time she met a young man who seemed to know about the free life. "Let me help to liberate you," he said, putting his arm around her. And so they went to his van and drove to a vacant lot where the young man kissed her and "liberated" her and told her to leave and drove away.

Many days later — days that passed without recognition or remembrance — the girl found herself sitting on a bench waiting for a bus in the middle of the desert. As she sat there gazing at the distant mountains, conscious of little more than the rising heat, she heard herself say, "I don't know what to do."

"Whatever you do will be foolish," said a voice from behind her.

"What?" the girl asked with some surprise, not sure whether she was listening to a person or a hallucination. The voice was that of an old woman with bony hands.

"Good decisions come from good values," continued the old woman, as she watched her knitting rather than the girl. "You have thrown your values away and so your decisions are poor."

"But I wanted to be free," the girl answered.

"There is no freedom without values," the woman said. "Without values there is only slavery."

"You know nothing about me," said the girl, her anger rising. "I'm not a slave to anyone. And I can do anything I want to. So just be quiet."

As she got on the bus to yet one more destination, the girl turned back to the old woman and said, "I'm sorry I got mad. The truth is, I'd do anything to be happy for one hour."

"That pretty well sums up your entire problem," the old woman said.

✠✠✠

Two Conversations on Direction

And then you turn here to the right."

"Really? No, I don't think so. The left path must be the way. It's more attractive, and it somehow just feels right."

"I'm sorry, but you have to take the fork to the right. See the little sign pointing the way?"

"Yes, but something just tells me the left fork is the one to take. The ground looks better, and that tree up ahead seems so persuasive."

"Well, I ought to know the way to my own house. There is only one way, along the right path."

"Uh uh. The right path looks bad. I just can't believe it leads to your house. You probably don't remember correctly."

"You'll get lost if you don't come this way. The other fork dead ends. The only thing there is a swamp, a pit, and a snake."

"It can't be. It looks so well traveled. And I have such a feeling that it will take me to your house; I've got to try it."

⌘ ⌘ ⌘

Hi. Hop in."

"Thanks, I appreciate the ride."

"No problem. Where are you going?"

"I don't know. That's what I want to find out. Where are you going?"

"To San Diego."

"Then where are you going?"

"Back home, why?"

"And then where are you going?"

"Well, oh, I get it. Then I'm going to rise in the firm and become president."

"And then where will you go?"

"I guess eventually I'll retire. Say, you feeling all right? You seem a little strange."

"But after you retire, where will you go?"

"Well, we all die eventually, so I guess I'll wind up at the cemetery."

"And then where will you go?"

"I get it. You're one of those religious fanatics, right? I think you'd better find another ride. You can get out here."

"Okay, I'm going. But I see you don't know where you're going, either."

"Yes, I do. I'm going to San Diego."

✠✠✠

SEMIOTICS STRIKES OUT

It so happened in heaven one day that two souls who had been friends in their college years on earth met after long lives apart. After a few minutes of joyous reunion and recounting of their lives, one of the souls realized that they were now in a place where all hearts can be revealed, and where they no longer needed to hide anything.

"You want to hear something funny, Lissa?" the soul said. "Back when we were young, I really loved you. Not having you for my wife is the one great regret of my earthly existence. Pretty silly, huh?"

"Not at all," said Lissa. "I always secretly loved you, too, and hoped against hope that someday you might notice me."

"Why didn't you say anything?"

"I was too shy. But I sent you hints."

"Hints?"

"Yes, like the brownies I gave you that rainy day in the student union."

"Oh, or like the chocolate-chip cookies you gave me that one time?"

"Well, no, those were only cookies. I was just being friendly. But that Christmas when I gave you a coffee mug. That meant I loved you."

"Oh, I know. That thank-you note you wrote when I fixed your sink you signed, 'Love ya special.' That was a hint, huh?"

"Actually, I signed all my cards and notes that way, so I was just thanking you then. But remember that note I wrote where I called you a 'weird monster man'? Boy, how I loved you then. I wish you'd responded."

"I thought maybe that meant you didn't like me. I never was good at hints. I remember thinking a few times that some girl was hinting that she liked me but when I would ask her out or mention romance, she'd always look shocked and be dumbstruck with disbelief that I could ever have thought she'd be interested in me." And here the soul sighed, as only souls can sigh.

"Well, why didn't you just say something to me, like, 'I love you'?" asked Lissa.

"I was afraid. And I didn't want to risk destroying our friendship by producing unwelcome romantic overtures. And besides, I sent you hints, too."

"Your overtures, as you call them, wouldn't have been unwelcome. But what do you mean you sent me hints?"

"I took you out to lunch."

"But you took lots of girls out to lunch."

"That was just for companionship or friendship. I just liked them, but I loved you. I thought about you day and night all through college, and for awhile after graduation, too."

"I wrote you a couple of love letters that I never sent."

"Gosh, I wish you'd said something."

"I wish you'd said something, too."

⌘ *As we pass through earthly life so quickly and only once, how sad that our fear of rejection is so often stronger than our love.*

✠✠✠

Seeing is Believing

One day an idle young man was wandering through the woods not far from his town when he happened upon an old woman standing around a rather smoky fire and stirring a kettle. Being the modern young man that he was, he immediately blurted out his first impression:

"Gosh, you're ugly and whatever you're cooking stinks," he told her.

"Well, if you don't like my looks," answered the old woman, "I can fix that." She then spoke a few strange words, which were followed by a dramatic puff of smoke, and the young man discovered, not that the old woman had transformed herself into a beautiful young maiden, but that the young man could no longer see.

"Now I've protected you from all ugliness and every unpleasant sight," said the woman. "And you'll remain this way until you can find someone to marry you. And it will have to be someone who can look beyond externals better than you, because I'm also changing your looks a bit." Here the woman gave a little laugh and uttered a few more unintelligible words. Soon there was another puff of smoke.

"Ooh, bummer," said the young man, feeling of the new bump on his nose and the deep wrinkles now in his cheeks.

When the young man returned to town, he quickly discovered that his social life was now pretty much a historical artifact. Whenever he went to a party, the reaction was always the same.

"What's wrong with him?" some girl would ask.

"He's gotta look that way until someone marries him," would come the reply.

"Hasn't that plot already been done?" the girl would say, walking off in another direction.

But, hey, this is a fairy tale and I'm in a good mood so let's say that finally, after many rejections, the young man found a nice girl who actually loved him as he was.

As the young man got to know her, he kept trying to imagine what she looked like. After awhile, he constructed a picture of her in his mind, so that whenever he looked in her direction, his imagined vision of her came before his eyes so vividly that he felt he could almost see her. He thought that he could very nearly see the slight curve of her lips, the sunlight shining in her hair, the expressions of delight or concern on her brow.

Well, anyway, things worked out so well that pretty soon the girl's father was mortgaging his house to pay for the wedding.

When the bride and groom awoke on the first day of their honeymoon, the young man discovered that his eyes had been opened. However, he also discovered that the girl lying beside him did not have the deep blue eyes with long eyelashes, or the upturned nose with little freckles of the girl he had been seeing in his mind. The young man, still in the habit of blurting out his first impression, said, "Gosh, you've changed."

"No," said his new wife. "The only thing that's changed is that now you can see. Oh, and you no longer have a bump on your nose."

"But where's your blonde hair?" the young man asked.

"My hair has always been this color," the girl said, fingering her chestnut tresses.

"But you look so different," the young man said, still confused.

"When you looked at me before," the girl explained, "you saw only your imagination. This is what I'm really like."

"I see," said the young man, as he embraced her and began to give her a thousand kisses.

"I know," she said.

✠✠✠

A Traditional Story

Once upon a time, several time zones from your house, there lived a king who had tons of money, mansions and castles on too many lots, plenty of art and cultural treasures, dozens of wives (some of whom loved him), and so much power that the mere mention of his name caused cardiac arrest among a considerable number of his subjects. But—he was not happy. So he called his advisors to him to seek their advice.

"My soul troubles me," he told his court. "I have seemingly a full life, but I do not find happiness here. In the middle of an amusement, or when I wake at night, or as I take a bite of rare and delicious food, I feel an overcast sky in my heart. Help me to dispel this cloud."

"Perhaps your majesty would be happy if he had more wealth," suggested his treasurer. So the king increased the taxes on his people, hired traders to go to distant lands to buy and sell, told his workers to redouble their efforts in his precious metals mines and minted more coins than ever. It wasn't long before the king had so many storehouses full of treasure that he couldn't even count them.

On many an occasion his majesty would be riding through a city and see a huge building he didn't recognize, and upon inquiry, discover that it was yet one more warehouse full of his loot. And let me tell you, these warehouses were so glutted with gold and jewels and coins and rich carpets and Old Master paintings and antique vases that when the king wanted to look inside one, the jewels would flow out the door like gravel and the coins would spill out like water. His servants got so tired of replacing the excess that they finally just began to shovel it into the trash can after the king left. (Of course, they probably helped themselves to a little bit of it, too.)

In his palaces, the king had so much fancy stuff that ancient statues were used as door props in the stables, thousand-year-old urns were used as spittoons in the kitchen, and scraps of precious carpets were used to clean the servants' boots. The point is that after all this additional acquisition, the king's lifestyle was much fancier, but the king himself was still not happy.

"What his majesty needs is activity," said the king's culture minister. "Activity is the rubbing paper that scours the rust from the soul and burnishes her to a new shine. If the king would just engage in some hobbies, he would find contentment." So the king took up some hobbies: hunting, painting, dancing, building (more mansions and castles), eating, woodworking, stamp collecting, riding (in his golden carriage and on horseback), swimming (in his pool full of pearls), and even knitting. In all he tried thousands or perhaps hundreds of activities, each of them dozens of times.

He also held athletic contests, built amusement parks, and ransacked the world for jugglers and magicians and singers and players and storytellers (that's how I met him) and musicians. He ate too much, drank too much, and danced and played and watched and traveled and did too much and basically engaged in a constant frenzy of activity from morning to night, from January to December, from the beginning of the decade to its end. And the result was that he was amused for awhile, but was mostly fat and tired and sometimes drunk and often disoriented, but still not happy.

"Perhaps your majesty would be happy if he ruled the surrounding lands and felt secure from attack," suggested the head of his army. "For the proverb says, 'In security lies happiness.'" So his majesty instructed his generals to go forth and conquer the territories around him. After a preposterous quantity of noise, smoke, blood, guts, and dying, the king found himself in possession of jillions of acres of farms and towns and houses and cottages and the souls of all those who lived therein. He now ruled over the land as far as he — or even someone with good eyesight — could see in every direction from the top of his highest tower. At any time of day or night the king could call for the relief of a distressed friend or the beheading of an enemy. He had absolute say over the life or death, the happiness or suffering, of millions of people of every rank and degree, from the most exalted noble in a seaside mansion to the most unfortunate street urchin in a grimy and stifling hovel. Such a thought sometimes gave the king half a smile, but he was still not happy.

"Perhaps what the king needs is love," said the eunuch in charge of the king's harem. "If he would marry a new variety of ever more beautiful wives, he would perchance find happiness among them." So the king decided to realize this scenario in three dimensions and searched throughout his kingdom for the most desirable women he could find. He found pretty ones and witty ones and laughing ones and moody ones and smart ones and elegant ones and plain ones and philosophical ones and decorated ones — women of every proportion, size, color, personality, and talent, and he married a hundred of them, some of whom loved him even more than those among the first few dozen he was already married to. And the king found much pleasure in his wives, but he was still not truly happy.

"The king will find happiness only in wisdom," said one of the king's scholars. "For it is written that 'truth is a joy unto itself.'" So the king applied himself to books of wisdom, and to seeking the knowledge of all his many scholars and sending throughout all his realm to find the wise from every land. Dozens came and dozens pretended to instruct him in wisdom or in the way to happiness, but while he found some really good advice and some satisfying rules for life, happiness still eluded him.

Then one day came a woman from a land beyond the sunrise. Her words were few but they so affected those who listened that she was immediately granted an audience with the king, who explained the discontent of his condition.

"Here before me," he said, "it would seem that I have everything a man could want. I have three or four rings on every finger, I can caress a beautiful woman's hair in any color, I can ride a week in any direction and find my statue erected and feared, and I can hear any melody or see any play at my command. I possess or can do or enjoy everything I can imagine, and everything that the most creative of my servants can imagine. And yet I find that happiness is nowhere to be found. I am always rankled by a feeling of dissatisfaction and haunted by an awareness of emptiness."

"Truly, his majesty's desires seem to be infinite," said one of his courtiers, scarcely more able to hide his disgust than his envy.

"His majesty's desires are indeed infinite," said the woman. "For that is the nature of the human heart. The heart's deepest desires cannot be satisfied by any finite thing."

"Then what am I to do?" asked the king with dismay.

"You must seek the Infinite," the woman said.

"And where can I find it?" he asked. "What form does it take?"

"The Infinite is not a thing or in a particular place," said the woman. "But seek Him and you will find happiness."

When the people saw that the woman was returning to her land, they asked what she had said to the king.

"She reminded us of what we had forgotten," said one of the king's scholars, "that we are but travelers through an ephemeral landscape, and that on a journey through a desert, we should not expect to find happiness from fingering the grains of sand in the dunes. We find happiness by finding our way home."

✠✠✠

THE DAY CREATIVITY MET THE LINEAR DRAGON

It was a winter's rainy day when the new Vice President for Design Concepts (who had just been promoted from Senior Accountant because he could calculate to the nearest nickel how much a new car would cost to build) noticed that two of his employees, a young man and a young woman, were not at their desks. Upon inquiring, he was told that they had "gone to the loft to be creative." The Vice President (who could remember the part number of every component he had ever touched) calmly adjusted his bow tie, cleared his throat, checked to see that his shoelaces were still tied, and then strode briskly down the long corridor of the half-remodeled automobile factory. Soon he was walking up the stairs to the loft, only to arrive at a door marked, "Do Not Disturb."

Viewing the sign as an affront to his authority, he applied Chapter Two of the assertiveness training book he had just finished and quickly opened the door with determination and a scowl.

What he saw was not what he expected. Near the door was a boom box, playing very lively but not overly loud classical music. Directly in front of him across the room he saw the young woman, barefoot and wearing, instead of her business attire, purple sweatpants and a torn green sweatshirt. Worse than this, she was turning cartwheels and saying what sounded to him like, "Put it in the lake, dip it, water proof it, French dip it, soak it, drench it, pinch it, wrench it." When she stopped to attend to his interruption, he noticed that her hair was rubber banded into a vertical column on top of her head.

The young man was sitting off to one side, wearing jeans and a T-shirt printed with the words, "None of the Above." Nearby was an open ream of copier paper, many sheets of which he had evidently wrinkled up into a ball and tossed at a trash can a few feet away, with highly indifferent accuracy. A few of the sheets had been written on with multicolored felt-tip pens and placed carelessly in several piles.

"What's going on here?" demanded the Vice President.

"We work here," said the young man.

"Not any more you don't," said the Vice President sternly. "Just what do you think you're doing, anyway?"

"We're working on the new Blister DLX," said the young woman.

"I don't see any work being done here," the Vice President shot back.

"We're thinking," the young woman said.

"This doesn't look like thinking to me."

"Oh? And what does thinking look like to you?" asked the young man.

"Well, it certainly doesn't look like this. This is goofing off — and stop wasting that paper. Who are you, anyway?"

"I'm Scott and this is Tina," the young man said. "We're creative analysts. We're working on cost-cutting ideas."

"Cost cutting?" sneered the Vice President. "You don't even have a calculator. And besides, we've got engineers and accountants to cut costs, so even if you were doing that, you'd be either superfluous or redundant. I want you out of the plant by this afternoon."

That afternoon Scott and Tina went to the Vice President's office. As Scott stretched out on the floor and began to spread out a few papers, Tina pushed aside many feet of adding machine tape and sat in the Lotus position on one end of the Vice President's desk. The Vice President was not quite so upset that he did not notice that Tina was wearing earrings made from crumpled balls of paper hanging from bent paper clips. "We'd like to ask you to reconsider your firing us," said Tina. "We have some good ideas for the Blister."

"Get out," said the Vice President.

The next day all the executives met at a regularly scheduled administrative meeting, where there seemed to be some confusion and delay in getting started. Finally, the President of the company spoke up. "I'm sorry for the delay," he said, "but we had scheduled a report on cost saving ideas by two of our top creative analysts and it now appears that some idiot fired them yesterday. However, we are in the process of getting everything straightened out, and they should be here soon."

"I hope it's Scott and Tina," one of the other executives said. "They're really brilliant."

"If unconventional," noted another.

"Unconventional or not," said the Chief Operating Officer, "I'll never forget how they saved us eighty-six million dollars on the Dazzle II by helping us reduce the number of parts. And when their expense account came through, all they'd bought were radio batteries and a couple of reams of paper."

"I remember that," said the first executive. "No fancy research, no costly experiments, just pure thought, just great ideas. They actually know how to think."

"What kind of a jerk would fire people like that?" someone asked.

And so it was that the new Vice President for Design Concepts was invited to take his skills to some other company, even though he could recite the exact cost of every part of every car the corporation made.

✠✠✠

THE WALL AND THE BRIDGE

In the high country of a far away land there once stood a massive wall, blocking the pass between two mountains. Just below the wall was a path leading around the mountains—a path made possible by a bridge connecting it across a deep chasm directly in front of the wall.

Now, the wall and the bridge were always bickering. One day when an old peddler leading an even older mule with a load of shabby wares crossed the bridge on the way to a distant fair, the wall said to the bridge, "You know, the trouble with you is that you have absolutely no discretion. You let just anyone walk over you. In fact, you're the slut of architectural forms, granting promiscuous entry to all and sundry."

"Is the greenness I see all over you moss or envy?" replied the bridge. "I enable people to fulfill their dreams; I provide opportunity for a better life. You're just an obstructionist, but I'm a facilitator—a metaphor for access, for hope, for possibility."

On another day a young maiden fleeing evil men ran across the rocks until she reached the wall where she could go no farther. She cried out and pounded her fists against the wall in despair until the men caught up with her and carried her away. The bridge then said to the wall in disgust, "You once accused me of having no discretion, but you are worse, for you are completely heartless. You're so cold and rigid that you cruelly prevent even the distressed and needy from passing by. Maybe that's why walls are known everywhere as symbols of 'No!' while we bridges are known as symbols of 'Yes!'"

"You, my loose and easy friend," said the wall, "indeed let the distressed pass, but you also let the criminals pass. I, on the other hand, provide the needed security to keep the land behind me safe from harm. I am a protector, and I defend this pass and the country well."

This dialogue continued for many years until one morning when suddenly the earth shook with great violence. So strong was the tremor that both the wall and the bridge were reduced to rubble at the bottom of the chasm. Not many months later men came to repair the damage. In the process of reconstruction, however, the stones that were once part of the bridge were used to rebuild the wall and the stones that were once part of the wall were used to rebuild the bridge.

"Now I'll show you what a wall should really be like," said the new wall. "It shouldn't be cold and rejecting to everybody." And so at first, the new wall let many people climb up over it.

"And I'll show you what a bridge should do," said the new bridge. "It shouldn't let just anybody across." And so at first, the new bridge provided a difficult passage, causing many travelers to trip on the surface and a few even to fall over the edge.

But as spring and summer, harvest and winter came and went again and again, the rocks on the new wall grew more and more slippery and the little projections gradually broke away, so that climbing over or even getting a foothold became very difficult. And in the same passage of time, the rough spots on the new bridge wore down and the crevices filled up, so that passage across became much easier.

"You see," said the new bridge to the new wall, "you've learned something about being a wall."

"Well," the new wall replied, "I've known all along

that I must guard the pass and fortify the defenses of the country. And of course I know it's my job to keep out all those who don't belong. But I see you've finally discovered how to be a bridge."

"You can say what you like," answered the new bridge. "But I've always understood that I provide a critical link in the path around the mountains, and that my purpose is to help travelers across the gorge."

As the years collected, as years do, the new bridge and the new wall began to think less and less about what they had once been and more and more about the task they currently had to do, until eventually it became impossible for anyone to tell that the new wall had once been a bridge or that the new bridge had once been a wall.

"How indiscriminate and common you are," the new wall would often tell the new bridge.

"And how inflexible and repressive you are," the new bridge would reply.

✠✠✠

THE WISH

While walking along the beach one day, a man spotted an old, barnacle-covered object which on closer examination he discovered to be an ancient bronze oil lamp. "Hah! Aladdin's lamp," he thought, jokingly. "I'll rub it." To his surprise, when he did rub it, a genie appeared.

"Okay, Bud," said the genie, in a remarkably bored tone. "You have one wish—anything you want. What is it?"

"Money," the man said instantly, his eyes widening. "Yes! Endless money. Riches! Wealth! Ha! Ha! Huge, massive, obscene wealth!"

"I thought so," said the genie in the same bored tone.

"No, wait," the man said, his eyes suddenly narrowing. "Power. Yeah, that's it. Complete and total power over everyone and everything in the world. With power I could get all the money I wanted."

"So you want power, huh?" asked the genie.

"Well, yes," said the man, now a bit hesitant because of the genie's less-than-enthusiastic tone. "Of course, with money I suppose I could buy power. Which do you think I should ask for, Genie?"

"How about world peace or personal humility or an end to famine or maybe an end to greed," suggested the genie, emphasizing the last phrase. "Or perhaps the gift of discernment or knowledge or spiritual enlightenment or even simple happiness."

"But with money or power I could buy or command all those," objected the man.

"Yeah, sure," said the genie.

"Well, just give me power and I'll show you that I can have everything else, too."

"You shall have what you ask," said the genie resignedly. "Whether you shall have what you imagine you must learn for yourself, and you will soon find out."

"Well, I certainly hope to have it all. Don't you ever hope, Genie?"

"Yes," said the genie. "I hope that someday my lamp will fall into the hands of a wise man."

And so the man was given power over everything on earth, over every government, every event, every activity of every soul. As a result, his name was soon pronounced with hatred and contempt by everyone, and in a few months he was assassinated by his most trusted followers.

✠✠✠

Several One Way Conversations

"Yes, they are shackles, but they are made of gold," said the man, as he asked for another pair on his wrists and two more on his ankles.

⌘ ⌘ ⌘

"You can see how great I am by observing what I have done," said the chisel to the other tools, as they gazed upon the beautiful statue.

⌘ ⌘ ⌘

"My word is as good as my check," said the forger, as he handed over partial payment and promised to pay the balance later.

⌘ ⌘ ⌘

"May you get everything you want," said the philosopher to his enemy, knowing that his enemy would not recognize his words as a curse.

⌘ ⌘ ⌘

"I'll teach this dirt not to muddy my shoes," said the man, shoveling madly, only soon to discover himself in a pit.

⌘ ⌘ ⌘

"Now I see how essential material things are," said the man, as he looked at the ashes of his burned down house.

⌘ ⌘ ⌘

"How dare you, who are nothing but a low worm, to try to tell me what to do," said the man, as he stood there unmoving, just before the piano landed on him.

✠✠✠

HOW THE KING LEARNED ABOUT LOVE

Back in the days of knights and chivalry and courtly love, a beautiful young woman fell in love with a man of noble birth, who, however, was already married. Their love continued to grow until the woman granted and the man took more than virtue could properly countenance and one morning the woman awakened with the right to use the pronoun "we" whenever she spoke.

She realized that she could not inform her lover because of his position, for he was not only married but also a very prominent member of the court. So she concealed the matter remarkably over many months, until, in the fullness of time, it could be concealed no longer. At that point she resolved to throw herself on the mercy of her mistress, the king's daughter, to whom she was a lady in waiting. She took her newborn son to the princess and begged quite pathetically for her help.

The king's daughter, knowing that the king was a hard man who had never hesitated to crush, kill, or otherwise persecute anyone who offended him in the slightest, realized that she could not tell the truth or say simply that the child had been found during one of the princess' walks, because the king would then send it to a harsh life in an orphanage—and that would be if she found him in a good mood. She decided instead to declare to the king that the child was her own and take the guilt, together with any other consequences, upon herself, for she loved her lady in waiting very much.

When the king learned that his daughter had given

birth (or so he believed), he was unutterably furious, and spent the better part of an hour ranting and shouting execrations and breaking things. But when he demanded which of his knights had helped her into this situation, the princess, not willing to sacrifice any of the noble and completely innocent knights of the castle, invented the story of a secret lover from outside the castle walls.

The king suspected that his daughter was lying, or trying to lie—for the girl was so honest that she could not dissemble with conviction—so that he was now even more uncontrollably enraged than before; he now began screaming directly at his daughter and breaking larger and more expensive things. And because he could think of nothing but her duplicity and disobedience and his injured honor and her betrayal of his affection, he coldly (or rather hotly) determined to banish her from the kingdom. "For," he argued, "I will love not those who love not me." He therefore cruelly turned the girl and the child over to the traders of a passing caravan from a distant land who would take them past the borders of the kingdom.

Even as she saw her father's look of hatred as she was packed into the wagon at the rear of the caravan, the princess did not alter her resolve to keep her secret, for now she understood that if the king knew the truth, her lady in waiting would most certainly be executed. As for the lady in waiting, she was so stricken with grief over the king's actions that she very nearly took her own life. But the princess had commanded her never to reveal the secret, regardless of the consequences, and the lady in waiting feared that the princess would be exposed by such an action. So the woman, helpless to remedy the situation, instead fled the palace in tears.

As the traders proceeded out of the kingdom, the princess resolved that, whatever should happen to herself, she would not see the child grow up a slave. She therefore watched carefully for an opportunity and one night sneaked off from the traders as far as she could get in the cold and dark, and put the child near a hut, hoping and praying that it would find safety and a free life, however humble. She then sneaked back to the traders, and pretended to be cuddling the baby in her arms.

The caravan traveled two full days before her deception was detected. When it was, the princess once again played audience to violent anger. The traders yelled and cursed the girl; then they beat her with fists and even with sticks, accompanied by more curses and threats; but nothing they could do could force her to tell what she had done with the baby. The traders, remembering the promises made to them by the king to encourage the secrecy of their charges, and fearing the consequences of a breach of that secrecy, sent riders back over the route they had traveled, to search everywhere.

Meanwhile an old woodcutter, who lived in the hut with his wife, found the baby and brought it inside. As they looked upon the beautiful, healthy child, their eyes shone with a sparkle that they thought had long ago disappeared forever. But even in their delight, they recognized immediately that the child was no ordinary foundling, for it had noble features and was wrapped in silks and wore a gold brooch with a white lily on it.

They soon recognized that the child would need better fare than the rough crusts and ordinary water the couple subsisted on—for they were extremely poor—so they began to wonder how they could take care of it.

"We could pick some of our neighbor's fruit at night," suggested the woman, "or perhaps sell the gold brooch."

"Or we could cheat the king the next time he buys wood," said the woodcutter sarcastically. "But we won't do any of those things. You know that it isn't right to do wrong, even to bring good. God has brought us this child;

I pray that he will help us feed it."

Now, the old woodcutter had been saving a few coins from his meager earnings over the past three years in order to buy himself a new axe head in the spring. "But," he thought to himself, "I suppose I could sharpen this old head one more season, and with a little longer handle, it ought to be good enough to get my by." So he took the money he had saved and gave it to his wife, instructing her to buy the child proper food and raiment.

The old woman was so moved by this sacrifice that she took off her locket—other than her wedding ring the only piece of jewelry she owned, and an heirloom from her great grandmother, at that—and contributed it to the welfare of the child. "For," she said, "I was never so foolish as to believe that love had no price."

Just a few days later a rider from the traveling caravan arrived, and visited the woodcutter's neighbor. Because the woodcutter was not far away at the time, he overheard the conversation. "Have you seen anyone with a baby in the past week?" demanded the rider roughly.

"Who's asking?" asked the neighbor, without excessive politeness. As the woodcutter heard the angry, cursing, threatening reply of the rider, he ambled back to his hut to inform his wife of what was going on. The couple was quite shrewd enough not to reveal anything to a rude, angry, and ill-dressed man on horseback, because, they concluded that, however deficient their own hospitality to the child, it was likely to be better than whatever would be offered by such a ruffian. "And besides," the woodcutter's wife said, "I already love the child too much to give him up."

As the days passed, the old couple grew thoroughly attached to the baby. They both found themselves unexpectedly humming little tunes or smiling for no apparent reason, and they both found their chores suddenly lighter and easier. They worked faster, eager to finish and once again spend some time playing with the child.

However, it wasn't many weeks before the old wood-cutter and his wife were forced to admit that they were simply too old and too poor to raise the child as it should be, and that they ought in all fairness to the babe to find a better home for it. "For," as the old woman explained, "I love the child too much to keep him."

So the woodcutter took the child to a house where several holy women lived and, after explaining the brief history of the child as he knew it, asked for their help. "The wife and I don't have the learning behind us, the money with us, or the years ahead of us to raise this child as it ought to be raised," said the woodcutter to the matron of the house, "so we'd appreciate it if you could find it a proper home."

"Our small endowment provides us with only a modest living," the matron said, "but we will care for the child until we can find out whom it belongs to, or until we can find it a good home." So the man left the child with them and went on with his wood cutting. The matron of the house assigned care of the child to one of the newest of the holy women, who could nurse it.

About this season in the kingdom, the queen gave birth to a son also. The child, however, was weak and sickly, and failed to flourish. In just a few weeks it developed a fever and died suddenly in the night. The queen, in addition to her grief, was frantic with anxiety, knowing that the king was such a hard man that if he knew his only son had died, he would hate the queen and perhaps divorce her. So she sent, with the utmost secrecy, a trusted servant to find another child to replace the one she had lost. "Bring me a child with no past," she told her servant, "and I will give it a future."

Finding such a child was a tiring and frustrating task

for the servant, and he met with humiliation and rejection and insult and false leads and failure at every turn. But since this story is not about him, nor about the rewards of perseverance, let us say simply that eventually he found himself at the door of the holy order of women we have mentioned above.

"Yes, we do have such a child as you seek," the matron told him. "We were keeping him until we could find his parents, or until we could find him a good home. Perhaps your mistress, whoever she is, will care for him well." The servant assured the matron that this would be so and gave her a large gift to maintain the house and its charitable work. As she handed him the child, she said, "The woman who has been nursing the child says that this parting is like a death to her, for she has become very attached to him. But she loves him too much to think of her feelings. I hope that what is a sadness for her will be a happiness for the child."

"Truly, good woman," replied the servant, "it is rightly said that the death of every fruit is the seed of new life. Every ending is also a beginning."

As the years passed, the baby grew up into a fine, strong young man. The king, who remained crusty and harsh toward everyone else, changed completely when his son (as he supposed) entered the room. The king became actually friendly and laughed some and often engaged in animated conversation with the young prince. The king was often heard to say that he would never let the prince part from him even for a day but that the prince should be his always. They often rode on horseback through the forest all day or sat together by the fire until the servants fell asleep, discussing the kingdom and enjoying each other's company.

When the prince reached his early manhood, the king not only took him into confidence on affairs of state, but began to share power with him, knowing that not many more years would pass before there would necessarily be a new king. Many of the king's decisions were now submitted to the prince before they were made, and the prince, to his credit, frequently moderated the king's stern and often cruel decrees.

By this time, the queen was in poor health, troubled by constant pain and a lingering cough. Everyone at the court eventually recognized that she was about to die. For several days the queen debated with herself whether or not to let the secret of the prince die with her, but at last, showing the heritage of her daughter's honesty, she decided that she must reveal it to the king.

By the time she reached this decision, the queen was truly on her deathbed, so she called the king to her and sat up weakly. "My king," she began, "I have a matter to disclose to you that has burdened my heart for many years. It concerns the prince." And here she hesitated for a few moments. The king waited in silence. "You," she continued, "are not his father."

The king, immediately concluding that the sanctity of his marriage bed had been violated, exploded into a rage that would likely have ended the queen's suffering prematurely had she not added as loudly as she could, "And I am not his mother." The king then, though still in shock, calmed himself enough to hear her explanation of the death of their natural son and her subterfuge in adopting the child who was now the prince. The king at first gave little credit to this tale, thinking that the queen was either delirious or scheming against him and his beloved son in some way. But he sent attendants to the holy order to discover the truth. They soon returned with the matron of the house and the woman who had nursed the prince as a baby.

"If what the queen tells me is true," said the king, "I

have no happiness, no reason to live. For the only thing I love has been taken away."

The matron from the holy order solemnly attested to the truth of the queen's story. "The prince was indeed the baby given us by the woodcutter so many years ago," she said. As the king felt a wave of despair washing over him, the nurse from the holy order came forward and spoke.

"With all deference to my Lady and to her majesty," she said, "the queen is only half correct. For the child was indeed not hers, but he is the king's son." She then pulled back the cowl of her robes, took down her hair and showed the king her face. Even through the ravages of two decades, the king could still clearly see the face of his daughter's lady in waiting, his lover who had borne his child without his knowledge so many years ago. The lady briefly explained what had happened then and how she had immediately recognized the child when the woodcutter brought it to the holy house.

"You willingly gave me your son, even though I was evil?" the king asked in disbelief.

"I loved you," the lady in waiting said simply. "And I loved my son — our son — more."

When he realized how unjust and hypocritical he had been toward the lady, the princess, and the queen, the king was so overwhelmed with shame and humiliation that he fell to his knees and began pulling on his hair and sobbing loudly. His crying was the only sound in the room until the queen spoke.

"I forgive you, my husband and my king," she said. "And I love you."

"You love me?" the king asked, rising and turning to his wife with astonishment. "You love me after I have banished your daughter and proven unfaithful to you?" But there was no answer, for the queen had already closed her eyes for the last time.

The king stood as one who had been stunned. He could not speak or think. As he sat down in a stupor at the foot of the queen's bed, the prince suddenly spoke. "I have found a mother today," he said. "I must now find a sister, too. I shall leave immediately in search of her."

"No!" the king yelled, standing up. But then, recollecting himself, he said, "No, you're right. You must go from me and find your sister."

In the days to come, as the king sat alone in his richly tapestried rooms, he had many hours to think over the events that had formed his life and to ask himself whether there was not in love some quality that can be shown only in sacrifice, not in advantage; only in surrender, and not in triumph.

✠✠✠

The Fly and the Elephant

A fly sat on an elephant's back. When the elephant shuffled down a dirt road, the fly said, "What a dust we are making!"

When the elephant trudged knee-deep in the mud, the fly said, "How heavy we are!"

THE MAN WHO TALKED BACKWARDS

There was once a bizarre old philosopher who always seemed to say the opposite of what those who sought his advice expected. So contrary were his words that he was known as The Man Who Talked Backwards. His blessing on those he loved was, "May you have difficulty in this life," and his bitterest curse on his enemies was, "May your life pass without a single sorrow." Whenever someone asked him what course of learning to undertake in order to increase his knowledge, the philosopher would reply, "If you want to learn something, become a teacher." Whenever some grateful hearer would ask how he could repay the philosopher for his advice, he would always answer, "The best way to repay a debt to me is to cancel a debt owed to you."

The Man Who Talked Backwards reversed even the most common of proverbs. Instead of repeating that "to love is to be patient," he would always quote, "To be patient is to love." Rather than noting that "seeing is believing," he would say, "Believing is seeing." For, he explained, what you believe controls what you see.

A young woman once asked him, "What can I do to make someone my friend? Shall I oil my skin or brush my hair?"

"Rather you should oil the skin and brush the hair of the one you like," answered the philosopher.

Another day a young scholar approached The Man Who Talked Backwards and asked him what books he should read, "For," the student said, "I realize that the more I read the more I will know."

"You will indeed learn something by reading," answered the philosopher, "but the more you read the less you will know. That is what makes reading of value."

"But how shall I know what beliefs I should hold in order to live the best life?" the young scholar asked.

"You think that your beliefs shape your actions," replied the philosopher, "but I tell you, it is your actions that shape your beliefs."

One day a woman came to the Man Who Talked Backwards for advice. "I know," she said, "that 'to live is to choose,' so I have come here to discover how I might fix my choices to live a fuller, more productive life."

"The better saying," said the philosopher, "is that 'to choose is to live.' But if you want to live life more fully, do less."

"Do less?" the woman asked with surprise. "But I'm an achiever. I thrive on accomplishment."

"Perhaps you have already diluted your life into meaninglessness," suggested the philosopher.

"But I'm easily bored," said the woman.

"I am truly sorry," said the philosopher. "Did you ever seek help for yourself?"

"What do you mean?"

"For your infirmity of being bored."

"My infirmity?" asked the woman, again surprised.

"Ah," said the philosopher, "You attribute your boredom to others or to external circumstances."

"Well, of course," she said.

"In that case, I am sorry for your two infirmities."

"But I want to get as much out of life as I can," the woman protested. "You philosophers all say that one's life does not consist in material things because they disappear, but what then can I gain that I can keep?"

"The only thing that you can really keep—and keep forever—is what you give away," said the philosopher.

Late one afternoon a blunt young man came up to The Man Who Talked Backwards and asked him, "Now that you are old and about to drop dead, do you look forward to death or fear it—or perhaps I should ask, Did you live a good life or a bad one?"

"It is not one's life that determines his view of death," replied the philosopher, "but one's view of death that determines how he lives."

"So you are ready to end your life?" asked the blunt young man.

"Death is not an end to life, as you suppose," said the philosopher. "This world is but a mirror that reverses everything as it reflects it. Death therefore is merely the shattering of a mirror."

"Your mirror already has a large crack in it," said the blunt young man, with a laugh.

"Thank you," said the philosopher.

✠✠✠

THE CLUE

In every civilization, someone has to put up the signs
that guide us on our way.
— Proverb

Sometimes they had to drill the post holes up on Rocky Bluff—and it was a tough dig, what with the rocks and the hardness of the soil. They came home plenty tired and dirty on those days.

Other times they drilled the holes down in Sandy Meadow, where the augur slipped in smoothly, quickly, and easily. They all praised the meadow and said how great it was to get an assignment to put up some signs there.

And yet, when they told the stories of their lives—the stories that animated their faces and brightened their eyes—they always seemed to be speaking of Rocky Bluff.

✠✠✠

AN ANALOGY

As he clung to the sheer face of the rock, he could hear in his mind the voice of his climbing instructor: "If you make even a slight mistake, you will die instantly."

He knew then that he need not debate whether to be attentive in his climb. And he was glad also that God is like a rock only in his steadfastness.

✠✠✠

FOOD FOR THOUGHT

Once in the cafeteria of life a man made his choices from among the casseroles of culture and then entered the dining area to enjoy what he hoped would be the satisfaction of a meal of good taste. Because there were no completely unoccupied tables in the room, he selected one where the diners seemed reasonable, and, after an exchange of smiles of acknowledgment, he sat down and began to eat.

After a minute or two, as the man was just putting another particularly delicious morsel into his mouth, the diner sitting across from him caught his eye and said, "You eat too fast."

"Yes," said a woman nearby. "It's not healthy to gobble your food like that."

"In fact," added a third diner, "if you keep gulping your food down that way, you'll get indigestion — or worse."

"Well, I'm sorry," said the man, somewhat bewildered, "but I have always eaten like this."

"Well, then, you'd better learn to change," said the woman, "because if you don't slow down, you'll choke."

Now, whether the man was prematurely crotchety or just naturally perverse I cannot say, but it so happened that he decided to find an alternative set of dining companions rather than to adjust his lifelong eating habits. So he excused himself under the simple pretext of needing to search for a missing condiment, and, getting up, he went across the room to another table. After the usual civilities, he once again sat down and continued his meal.

It wasn't more than a few minutes, however, before the diner sitting next to him remarked, "You know, you're the slowest eater I've ever seen."

"Yeah," said a man across the table. "You eat so slowly your food will be cold before you're half done."

"Didn't your mother ever teach you not to dawdle over your food like that?" asked the woman to his left, somewhat severely.

"I'm sorry," said the man, in a slightly apologetic tone. "This is just the way I eat."

"If you can't learn to eat any faster than that, you'll be here all day," said one of the diners.

Once again the man decided that the better part of valor would be simply to move to another table rather than to change his natural eating rhythms.

Unfortunately, this particular table was already freighted with every condiment known to the virtuosos of culinary excess, so that the man was forced to invent an imaginary condiment before he could declare his need to go in search of it. And so, after an appropriate statement of intent, he rose to begin a pretended search for a nonexistent item. (And here we see that a search for the nonexistent is not always ineffective.)

As he walked away, he heard a voice from his now former table remark, "Not only is he the gold medalist of slow, but he's a very picky eater, at least for condiments. Give me some mustard and I'm good."

The man smiled as he crossed the room and joined the diners at yet a third table.

After a only a very small collection of minutes, the diner sitting across the table from the man smiled and said, "I'm glad to see you're eating so reasonably. Everybody else in here is eating either too slow or too fast."

"Yes," agreed another diner at the table. "Just look around. Some are chewing like cows on their cud, as if they've got all day, while others are eating like nervous chipmunks."

"And they're all so egocentric," added a third, "measuring others only by themselves."

"These are the only sane people in the room," the man concluded, continuing his meal happily.

✠✠✠

THE ASSAY

There once lived a king who delighted to take the measure of a man, so he often spent his days devising and indulging in calculated temptations. One day he called into his presence a wise man and a fool.

"Here are two goblets," said the king, "one of pure gold and the other of common clay. If you could choose to receive one, which would it be?"

"The gold one," said the fool.

"The gold one," said the wise man.

"It seems," said the king with some amusement, "that there is no difference between the wise man and the fool."

"Perhaps you should ask another question," said the wise man.

"Very well," replied the king. "Which of these two goblets is the better?"

"The gold one," said the fool.

"The question is ambiguous," said the wise man. "Better for whom? And in what way?"

"The cunning of the so-called wise amuses me," said the king. "But here is one last question: Which of these goblets would you rather drink from in your own home?"

"The gold one," said the fool.

"The clay one," said the wise man.

"Aha!" said the king. "The fool is more consistent than the wise man. For just now you said that you, O wise one, like the fool, would choose the golden goblet."

"With all deference, Sire," said the wise man, "your final question was not which would I accept from your hand, but which I would drink from in my home."

"All right," said the king, none too amused. "Unravel your subtlety."

"In my home," answered the wise man, "the clay goblet would deter me from an attachment to material things. As a gift to me, the gold one could be exchanged for a hundred of clay. For," he explained, "I have many disciples who have given up much for the sake of wisdom. Their pursuit of truth would not be circumvented by the acquisition of a clay drinking goblet. Those who thirst for knowledge also thirst for water."

The king was, of course, aggravated that he had failed to humiliate the wise man, so he sent both men from his presence. However, after a sleepless night thinking about his own possessions, he soothed his conscience by sending to the wise man the golden goblet, filled with rubies.

✠✠✠

DE MINIMIS NON CURAT LEX[3]

A man in the prime of life ate something quite disagreeable and died suddenly. However, his stomach later thought better of the food and the man awoke in his coffin. He banged his hands against the lid and cried, "Let me out."

"We can't let you out," said those in charge of his burial, "because you're dead."

"I'm not dead," protested the man. "I'm alive. Look at me." The attendants peeked into the coffin.

"You look like a corpse to us," they said.

"Then let me out and I'll walk around for you," said the man.

"We can't have a dead man walking around here," they protested. "It would hurt our business and possibly get us fired."

"Then get me a lawyer," said the man.

Soon there was a trial. The first to testify was the funeral master. "This man is trying to make a mockery of the dying process," he said, "and of the funeral business and of my long-respected house for the dead. He came here quite dead, and his burial is already scheduled. I have another burial this afternoon and cannot possibly delay this one or reschedule it. I humbly ask the court not to hamper the business of the living for the sake of the dead."

The next to testify was the doctor who had pronounced him dead. He stood up confidently before the court, barely allowing a passing scoff toward the recently dead man,

---

[3] "The law is not concerned with trifles."

and declared, "My medical degree comes from the most respected medical school in the country. I have more than 25 years of successful medical practice, serving many famous and wealthy patients. I have given presentations to medical societies and received numerous honors and awards. No patient of mine who has died in my care has ever changed his mind before. Not once. It has not happened before, it is not happening now, and it will not happen in the future."

The coroner then took the witness stand. "I am shocked," he announced testily, "that even for a moment anyone could even consider taking the word of a mere layman over that of a well-known expert. If for some completely unexplainable reason the court is able to overlook the tremendous reputation of the medical facility that employs me, willing to overlook—however recklessly—the fact that I was elected by a huge margin, if the court is willing to go to these extremes to indulge some upstart corpse devoid of any sense of duty in death, then I would simply say that I have examined 3,462 bodies in my career and that all were dead and all remained dead. No one has dared to challenge my authority like this."

Thinking that the evidence was perhaps too one-sided against the man, the judge ordered the man's relatives to testify. But they agreed with the previous witnesses that the man must be dead, citing as evidence that they had already moved into his house and begun to spend his money. The address changes had already been processed at the post office, and his newspaper already cancelled.

"I found him dead," said his widow, "and I grieved for him and said good-bye." She cited as proof an engagement ring from a new lover.

More than eleven other witnesses testified that they had all been told that the man was dead. "What do you have to say to this testimony?" the judge finally asked the man.

"Believe the evidence of your eyes and ears," said the man.

"That evidence is light when weighed against the evidence of tradition and reputation," said the judge. "It runs against what we all know. For when a man dies, who has seen him live again?"

And so the lid was nailed back onto the coffin and the man was taken to the cemetery, where, at length, the evidence of the court and evidence in the coffin were reconciled.

✠✠✠

THE MAN WHO PUSHED A ROPE UP HILL

It happened, as it sometimes does in remote and not thoroughly civilized kingdoms, that a man was arrested and sentenced to be executed for a crime so subtle that not even the king's advisers could delineate it with confidence. For this reason, the king pretended to be inclined toward leniency, but he alleged that he must devise some perfunctory test as a means of saving face. In truth, the king simply delighted in posing impossible tasks to his condemned prisoners, just to torture them with hope.

"Here is a piece of rope, shorter than you are tall," the king said. "Hear my promise: If, by this time tomorrow, you can push this rope up this small hill in a straight line, you will be free to go, loaded with gold and jewels, with silks and spices, and with a hundred servants carrying delicacies of your own choosing. If you fail to do this task, you must die."

The sky was beginning to cloud and the wind to rise, so the man prayed, "God, give me bright sunshine and a warm day in which to work." And the clouds dispersed and the wind grew calm.

The man struggled all day long to line up the rope and push on it. But however he pushed, the rope would bend to the right or to the left. When he pulled on the rope to straighten it, no matter how careful he was, the rope moved down the hill a little. The king, who looked from his window occasionally to see how the man fared, was roundly amused. When darkness had fallen, the man realized that he had lost more than three feet.

The man sat there, despondent in the dark, while the king stood at his window, smirking. "Why don't you pray again to your God?" he asked, punctuating his question with laughter. So the man thought he would.

"Oh God, help me to do this task," he said. "Only you can know how," he added, shaking his head slowly and sighing.

Not long after he prayed, the clouds began to return and the wind rose again. Soon a cold rain was falling and the man was quickly soaked to the skin. As the rain turned to snow, the man forgot his task and wrapped himself in his cloak as well as he could and waited for morning. The last thing he heard in that shivering night was the king's taunt, "My dear prisoner, your God certainly answers your prayers in a very odd way."

When morning came, the man awoke, almost surprised to find himself still alive in the icy silence. His clothes were frozen stiff. Looking with purposeless weariness over at the rope, he noticed that it, too, appeared to be frozen stiff. His eyebrows rose as he realized that the rope might be just stiff enough to push in a straight line. And it was.

✠✠✠

THE COST OF DISCIPLESHIP

Someone wanted to study philosophy under Diogenes. Diogenes gave him a dead fish to carry and told him to follow him. But the man for shame threw the fish away and departed. Later, when he saw the man again, Diogenes said, "The friendship between you and me was broken by a dead fish."
— Diogenes Laertius

Not so long ago in quite a modern town, a young man came to a wise man, sat down, and asked to be his disciple.

"Before you can become my disciple," the wise man said, "you must first answer one question."

"I will," said the young man.

"Hear, then, this story. A man found himself in a forest on a moonless night. His own nose was nowhere to be seen. Off in the distance he heard a child crying out to be rescued from a bear." The wise man paused to let the young man grasp the situation.

"And now the question," he continued. "Should the man rush toward the child, with no certainty of rescuing him, certain only that he himself will be injured by running into many trees and swampy bogs? Or should he wait until the revealing light of morning, when he can see to run straight to the child without hindrance or mishap?" The young man thought deeply about this question.

"I understand," he said at last. "The night is ignorance, where thoughtless impetuousness is punished by bruises and broken bones, if not death itself. In ignorance, one makes poor choices that result in harm. And I understand that the morning is the light of understanding, when one can see clearly to act well and teach truly. With enlightenment we can make better choices. My mind sees these things, and tells me of the value of the noble path to enlightenment, which I honor."

And here, the wise man gave a nod of acknowledgement.

"At the same time," continued the young man, nervously, "while my mind would choose according to the interpretation, my heart is so moved by the story — by the thought of a child in distress and immediate danger — that I would be compelled to suffer the unseen trees and bogs in an effort to rescue him. I know that is the wrong answer and I'm sorry." And he got up to leave.

"You may be my disciple," the wise man said.

✠✠✠

WHY MR. MINIVER HANGED HIMSELF

Mr. and Mrs. Miniver lived in a quaint old house on Allegory Road. Their house was well kept and their yard was beautiful, but Mrs. Miniver mostly frowned and Mr. Miniver mostly sighed.

One day when Mrs. Miniver came home from the store, Mr. Miniver put down his screwdriver and looked out the attic window. "Did we get something good for dinner when Mrs. Busy comes to visit?" he asked.

"*I* got something good for the dinner," answered Mrs. Miniver. "*I'm* the one who went shopping."

A little while later, a thought came to Mr. Miniver as he paid some bills in the upstairs study. "Emmie, dear," he said, "did we mail that invitation to Mrs. Busy yesterday?"

"*I* mailed the invitation," if that's what you mean," replied Mrs. Miniver.

It wasn't long before Mrs. Busy arrived for dinner. "Welcome, welcome," said Mr. Miniver, as he opened the door. "It's been so long since we drove out to see you."

"*We* drove indeed," said Mrs. Miniver. "If you recall, *I* did the driving."

Dinner proceeded and the three talked and ate and talked and talked. Mr. Miniver even managed to get in a whole sentence, short though it was. Mrs. Busy had just remarked on what a lovely place the house was, so Mr. Miniver commented, "We wanted it to look nice for you."

"And that's why *I* did all the cleaning," said Mrs. Miniver. "Honestly, Mr. M is the messiest painter on the face of the earth."

The next day when Mrs. Miniver got home from the store, Mr. Miniver was in the basement. But he had no question for his wife.

✠✠✠

THE DIRECTION OF WATER

One warm day in the early summer, a young boy came to visit his grandfather at his small cabin nestled among the trees just below the top of a large hill. The day was bright and pleasant, so they agreed to enjoy the outdoors and began a ramble down the hill, examining leaves and bugs and rocks and every kind of flower they encountered.

Soon they came upon a stream, fed by a natural spring bubbling up into a clear pool. The boy looked with wonder and interest as the water rose up through the sand and spilled out of the pool and down the stream bed. He watched carefully for awhile, as if he expected the wonder to cease. Finally, he asked, "Grandpa, how long will the water keep flowing?"

"This spring flows all year round," said the grandfather. "Through heat and cold, rain and drought, this spring is a faithful and dependable source of water."

"Where does the water come from?" asked the lad.

"A spring like this starts from high up there," the grandfather replied, pointing toward a mountain in the distance. "It begins with the rain and snow and the dew on the leaves of many plants, far up on the mountains. But that is only the beginning. These waters join together deep inside the earth, in the inner secret places, where they form a single, pure flow. The water must pass with great travail and great patience over long distances through sand and rock until finally, in the fullness of time, it rises forth from the earth here before us." The boy stood awestruck at this story until the grandfather broke the reverie by adding,

"You know, my boy, there is a great truth here: the greater the struggle, the purer the spring." The grandfather contemplated his own wisdom until it was the boy's time to break the meditation.

"Where does the water go, Grandpa?" he asked, looking down the stream. "I can't see it after it reaches that old log."

"There's another great truth," said the grandfather. "The only way to find where a stream will lead is to follow it."

So the boy and his grandfather followed the stream along its course down the hillside. They rambled at an easy pace, enjoying the song of the waters tumbling over the rocks in the stream bed and watching an occasional leaf or twig rush down the rapids of a particularly turbulent spot. They paused often to examine a curious vine or a rotting log or to touch the bark of a nearby tree or merely to look around them to see the forest at peace.

Eventually they came to the base of the hill where the stream stretched out along the plain. After walking awhile, they saw a place where, within the space of a few yards, the stream disappeared into the ground. "The stream ends here," said the boy. The old man said nothing but continued to stroll with the boy down the now dry stream bed, their feet crunching on the gravel in a most satisfying way. After many steps, the old man turned to the boy and said, "Why don't you dig a hole right there." The boy looked surprised for a moment, but soon began to dig in the bed. When he had dug down a foot or so, water seeped into the hole.

"There is water here!" the boy exclaimed, watching the level rise to a few inches.

"It's the stream," the old man said. "It has continued from where we last saw it, only now the gravel is on top."

"You mean the stream has been with us all along?"

asked the boy.

"That's right," said the old man, "and that's another truth you should remember: If you ever lose sight of a stream, and believe it has been lost, just look under the gravel and you will find it again."

✠✠✠

The Well

B ack in the old days a fresh, good-natured and rather beautiful girl decided that it was time for her to marry. But because she lived in an isolated house near a sparse village, her choice was limited—and not only limited, he wasn't yet mature enough to be serious material.

So the girl asked her mother for advice. "Why don't you go and sit by the well at the crossroads," her mother told her, "for that is where the young men come to find healthy and industrious wives. When a young man comes to the well, offer to draw water for him and he will like you."

"Very well," said the girl.

"However," the woman continued after a pause, "you don't want just any young man, but a man of discernment, one who can see beyond his eyes. You must therefore wear this cloak and this cowl and not show your face to anyone until he is curious enough to ask."

So the girl rose early in the morning, covered herself in the cloak and the cowl, and walked the distance to the crossroads, where she sat down by the well. The well was a busy place, with many people, young and old, men and women, coming to drink or draw water, but they all ignored the girl.

The girl was naturally cheerful and open-hearted, so she offered to draw water for old and young alike, and even for many women. For this the other girls mocked her. Whenever a nice young man did come, she offered to draw water for him, and he would often allow her, but he would not seem interested in her and would soon turn his attention to one of the other girls around the well, girls who knew just how to smile and giggle in the way that so transfixes young men.

As dusk began to turn into genuine night, the girl walked wearily home to her mother. "Many nice young men are less thirsty tonight on my account," she said, "but none spoke of romance, for they all looked with longing on the other girls, the ones they could easily see."

"Patience, my child," said the woman.

So the next day, and the next, and many following days, the young girl again rose very early and walked the long walk to the well at the crossroads, always wearing her cloak and cowl. And again she offered to draw for everyone who came to the well, whether for a deep and satisfying personal drink or a for large jar to take home to a thirsty family.

But every day, while the young men gladly drank her water, and occasionally held her hand in theirs as they tilted the ladle to their lips, none were curious enough to look under her cowl, for they all assumed that the girl had hidden herself because of her homeliness. So they offered their smiles to the less beautiful and less helpful but more visible girls around the well.

One evening after she entered her mother's house in the near darkness, she sat heavily in a chair and put her head down on the table in weary despondency. "Truly mother," the girl said, sighing deeply, "I think there is not in all the kingdom a man who can see beyond his eyes."

"Patience, my child," said her mother.

Many more days began and ended with long walks, with many pulls on the well rope, with the teasing laughter of the other girls in her ears; the girl's only comfort, which itself was punctuated here and there by a sigh, was the thought that she was being useful and the hope that she was learning patience.

Finally, in the heat of an ordinary afternoon, a dusty young man, who had arrived while the girl was busy helping someone else, threw himself down exhaustedly near the well and begged the girl for a drink. As was her custom, she drew him a full bucket of water and set it down next to him. She then took the ladle and helped him to drink. As with the other young men from countless days past, the young man attended closely to the water, and scarcely looked at her while he drank greedily.

When he had refreshed himself to such an extent that the girl had found it needful to draw a second bucket from the well, the young man turned to the girl and spoke. "Your servant's heart is greatly appreciated, for I owe you much, having been thirsty almost unto death."

"It is my pleasure to draw for you," said the girl simply. With that, the young man thanked her, took her hand, bowed, and — wished her well. (I know you're disappointed here, but I am trying to preserve some sense of reality, and besides, be patient and maybe eventually things will get better.) The walk home that night seemed particularly long and cold, and the girl was more downcast than usual, for she had liked the very thirsty young man.

When she arrived home and collapsed into a hard little chair, the girl announced to her mother, "I don't think I'm going to find a young man at the well — or anywhere."

"Patience, my child," said her mother. The girl was becoming impatient with these admonitions about patience, but before she could respond with irritation or disrespect, she fell asleep.

Several more days passed routinely and unremarkably, except for the debacle of the dog and the chickens, and that little incident about the big oaf who turned over the peddler's cart, but the girl scarcely noticed these. Even when a line formed on one especially hot day, where six or seven young men stood waiting to drink from her bucket, she was inattentive. She did notice the bucket becoming empty, though, and was about to let it down into the well again when a hand grabbed hers and prevented her.

"Here," a young man said. "Let me draw a bucket of water for you." She turned to him with surprise—for no one had ever before offered to draw for her—and immediately she recognized the dusty young man from a few days earlier, though he was not at all dusty now. As is usual with girls in situations like this, some feeling or other caused water to appear in her eyes, blurring her vision for a minute or two before it became copious enough to escape down her cheeks.

She thought she said, "Thank you," but she wasn't sure, but it didn't matter because the bucket was down, filled, and raised in a jiffy, and the next thing she knew after that was that she found herself drinking, for, almost to her surprise, she discovered that she had been quite thirsty herself.

The next thing she knew, or imagined, was that her mind was telling her that the words, "Will you marry me?" had appeared in her ears, quite unannounced. Her eyes opened (for she was one of those who drinks with her eyes closed) to confirm what she thought she had heard. There before her she saw the young man, on his knees, holding his hat over his heart.

"Are you willing to marry me, even though you haven't seen me?" her head made her ask, in spite of her heart yelling at her to say, "Yes!" loudly.

"But I have seen you," the young man said. "I've been watching you for several days. I've gotten quite a look at you, and your beauty has captivated me." Before the girl could reply, the young man continued: "Now then, let me see what face belongs to such beauty."

And with that, he pushed back the girl's cowl and

freed her tresses from her collar. I won't be coy about it — the young man was quite joyful to find that the girl he loved, whose true beauty he so admired, had such a handsome and likable face. In fact, the afternoon sun made her face shine with such warmth and her hair glow with such radiance that the young man was forced — he couldn't help it, I tell you — to push his hands, fingers spread, through her hair and to pull her lips to his, for at least an ample and generous minute. It is unfortunate that the girl was not wearing knee-high socks that day, for if she had been, the young man's kiss would have rolled them down all the way to her ankles for her, making it that much easier to take them off when she got home.

The girl's head and heart had another brief tiff, with the result that she said, "I will marry you, but you must also ask my mother." The young man promised to drop by on the morrow to talk to mom.

Now, if this were really a fairy tale, the young man would turn out to be a prince, arriving at dawn in a carriage drawn by twelve horses and accompanied by dancers and musicians. However, as you have certainly noticed, this story is a careful, historical account, and I must continue to record only the actual truth, without exaggeration or ornament.

The young man, in fact, was not a prince; he arrived the next day about ten o'clock, in a carriage drawn by only four horses, and was accompanied by only a single servant. True, he did own a decent castle, but with only a few hundred acres of land surrounding it. Even so, the girl's mother blessed the match anyway, and the two lovebirds were soon married.

Whether these two lived happily ever after or not, my sources do not inform me. (There's always a page missing when you want it most, isn't there?) The only clue we have about their married life is an obscure rhyme that at that time entered the lore of the neighboring villages and was sung by children at play for many generations afterwards:

Two buckets up, two buckets down.
Old thirst a dust, new never drown.

✠✠✠

THE CHOICE

A man decided to journey through the wilderness of life, so he went to a large stable to find a ride. He quickly chose a horse that looked strong and capable, and, leaping on, he spurred it hard. Immediately the horse leaped away and ran thunderingly out of control. It was a wild horse, crazy in the way only a few horses can be crazy, and it galloped past turns in the path, across trails, down embankments, and through the thick underbrush.

The man, who could barely even stay in the saddle, felt his clothing being ripped to shreds and his flesh torn and punctured by the rough, hostile bushes and branches. Finally he was thrown off onto a patch of rocky dirt, where he lay dazed and bleeding for quite some time. At length, he heard what sounded like his horse approaching, and not wanting to be stepped on, he wiped the bloody dirt from his eyes and looked up. The owner of the stable, who had arrived on another horse, was looking down at him.

"That will be ten thousand gold pieces," he said.

"What?" asked the man, confused by the shock of the fall, and half blinded by the sun. "That can't be true. Look what happened to me."

"When you chose your horse," the owner replied, "you didn't ask what it cost, so now you can't object to the bill."

"But I didn't think—"

"That's clear enough," interrupted the owner, "but you still must pay for the ride."

✠✠✠

INFORMATION UNDER LOAD

The boss sent his highly paid vice president to an expensive, week-long conference. The vice president listened attentively to every session but took only a few notes.

When the man returned, the boss asked, "What of importance did you learn?"

"Nothing," said the vice president.

"Okay, great," said the boss. "Thanks."

After the vice president left, the boss' administrative assistant could not contain her irritation any longer. "You just spent thousands of dollars to send your vice president to a conference, and when he comes back and tells you he learned nothing, you say that's just great?"

"Certainly," said the boss. "Our world is an information ocean where the worthy and the useless equally demand attention. Half the success of life is knowing what to ignore. In this case, the word *nothing* summed up five days of inessential data smog. I certainly got my money's worth. Now go make me a cup of coffee."

✠✠✠

THE AUTHOR OF OUR BEING

A new writing pen is always a joy," said the clerk in the stationery store. "And this model can produce broad strokes or thin lines, to create light impressions or a deep, bold impact. It is the identical model that has been used to write poetry and love letters, to sketch likenesses, and — why, it's even been used to write a peace treaty. The manufacturer's Quality Assurance team tests each pen individually by employing its best calligrapher to inscribe an entire paragraph on a sheet of superior quality paper."

The young mother was impressed by the sales presentation, so she bought the pen as a birthday present for her child.

The child ripped the package open eagerly and grabbed the pen in his fist. He then repeatedly jabbed it point first into the floor before he started to scribble on a piece of cheap construction paper. The ink bled, the lines grew thin and skipped, and finally the pen clogged and stopped writing completely.

"What a low quality pen," the mother said as she threw it into the trash can with disgust. "I was cheated."

⌘ *The wrong guide and the wrong purpose make even the best to fail.*

✠✠✠

Faculty Lounge

Not long ago, several professors sat down in the overstuffed chairs of the faculty lounge, and began to discuss the inability of words to communicate meaning.

Suddenly a young man burst into the room, and in a frenzied rush and with a terrified look, he shouted, "Run! Hide! There's an evil monster outside!"

"Nonsense," said the professor of semantics. "Evil is only a verbal construct without a concrete referent. Repetition and usage have convinced you that something unreal has existence. A common mistake for those whose lives are controlled by words." The young man stared at the professor with a look of astonishment.

"Allow me to demonstrate that I am not afraid of semantic inventions. After all, 'sticks and stones' you know." At this, the professor arose and walked out the door. A moment later the group inside the room heard a short scream followed by a crunching and slurping sound.

"You see?" said the hysterical young man, looking around at the others. "The evil monster got him."

"No, no, no, no, no," said the professor of sociology, somewhat patronizingly. "Evil is merely a social construct designed by the oppressor class—the bourgeoisie—to control the behavior of the proletariat and keep them down. And I refuse to be controlled." Upon which the professor got up and walked outside. Soon there was another short scream, followed by more crunching and slurping.

"Can't you see?" screamed the young man.

"You poor dupe," said the professor of postmodern literary studies. "You have been victimized by false consciousness. The concept of evil is an artifact of the late capitalist hegemony, imposing a totalizing narrative of absolutist moral bifurcation, designed to constrain your thinking to Western neocolonial categories. Everyone today knows the criticality of decentering such abhorrent truth claims through a deconstructive analysis of obtruded linguistic frameworks. And besides, whatever is out there would not be considered evil in many cultures, nor would it—or him or her—be smeared by the hyperjudgmental expletive, 'monster.'"

After this remark, the professor, clearly in a snit, walked to the exit, left the room, and slammed the door behind him. There was a brief cry of surprise, followed by more crunching and slurping.

"Evil! Evil I tell you!" was all the young man could say.

"Listen here, you judgmental and intolerant person," said the professor of ethics. "The concept of evil has long ago been denied ontological status in many thoughtful monographs. But you must know that even words without extant referents can harm others. A word like *evil* can scar someone for life. We must accept a variety of behavioral lifestyles and not be judgmental. We don't tell others what they can and cannot do. That's what tolerance is all about. After all, not everyone is just like us, but everyone needs acceptance. So, I'm going to go outside and give that person a big hug." And the professor of ethics did just that.

Those still in the lounge heard a brief but emphatic, "No, don't," followed by crunching and slurping, a bit slower, concluded by a burp.

"I've had enough of this charade," sneered the Women's Studies professor. "I'm going out to see what's really happening."

"Please, lady, don't go outside," pleaded the young man.

"You think you're clever, don't you?" said the professor. "But I can tell that this is just one more sick example of patriarchal oppression through linguistic enslavement. Men call things evil as a ploy to control women and keep them at home. 'Don't go outside,' they command. You want us all barefoot and pregnant in the kitchen, don't you? Food and sex, that's all we're good for, isn't it?" Before the young man could close his gaping mouth to begin a reply, the Women's Studies professor stomped out and slammed the door behind her.

Immediately there was the sound of a slap and a scream, followed by crunching and spitting.

"This amuses me," said the professor of multiculturalism. "The problem with you Westerners is that you do not realize that evil is *maya*, an illusion, a self deception. Your minds are still bound down to the remnants of the Judeo-Christian idea that evil is real. But evil simply does not exist for those with enlightenment."

"Okay, okay," said the young man in exasperation. "There's no evil monster outside."

"Yes," replied the professor of multiculturalism. "Now your cup begins to empty so that truth may enter."

"But there is a nice, man-eating creature outside. It will devour you if you leave the room."

"I imagine not," said the professor, who sauntered out the door.

The young man heard one or two crunching sounds, followed by a burp and a moan.

The faculty lounge was now nearly empty, and the young man, conscious of the failure of his warnings, sat down to think. But just then the door to the lounge blasted off its hinges and flew into the room. In the doorway stood a large, scale-covered green beast with a tremendously distended abdomen. The animal attempted a terrifying roar, but couldn't get it out. It did not look well. Then it groaned and fell over dead. The contents of its stomach, which consisted of the professors it had just eaten, emptied out onto the floor.

Looking at the disgorgement, the young man shook his head and said, "What an evil mess." Then he stepped over the corpse and went on his way, no longer afraid.

✠✠✠

IN THE PARK

I t was a bright spring afternoon at the university and many students had taken advantage of the weather to gather in the grassy area between the buildings. Some snoozed in the sunshine while others enjoyed a cup of coffee in the shade of one of the many very large trees.

Theodore walked past a group discussing a television series, a group discussing fingernail polish, and a group discussing campus football. He continued on his way until he overheard what sounded like an interesting conversation.

"There's no such thing as truth," a young woman with long brown curly hair was saying to her friends. Theodore stopped and looked at her as she spoke. "What passes for truth is just the temporarily dominant narrative, forced upon the world by the oppressor class." Even though, when she pronounced the words "oppressor class," she glanced back and forth at the men she was speaking to with an expression something less than friendly, Theodore noticed that this young woman had a look of intelligence on her face. But more than that, she bore a look of intensity and conviction. Her hair shook a little as she spoke, and she almost stomped her sandal-shod foot for emphasis.

"Transitorily enthroned subjectivity," said a young man in the group, evidently attempting to impress the young woman.

"Once the power structure shifts," the young woman continued, "a new hegemony is installed and the new, improved truth is forced on everyone." The young woman's sarcasm twisted her expression into a look of disgust, even as she flung her hands out in an open palm gesture for emphasis. Still, Theodore thought, she is rather attractive, in spite of her jeans with the holes in the knees and the T-shirt whose icon—which seemed to be an upheld fist—had been washed almost into invisibility.

Theodore thought the young woman was feeling disillusioned, though perhaps not yet bitter. There is always at least a slight sense of triumph and superiority in disillusionment, even when it results from the rejection of sacred values and the belief in absolutes like truth. She had, however, learned her philosophy well, whether from the books she read or the professors who taught her.

"Please excuse me, young people," Theodore said as he broke into the group. "But I find this young woman's talk very interesting. You see, I too am interested in truth, and you appear to have discovered something I did not know about it."

"Well, if it isn't a doddering remnant of the exhausted patriarchy," a spectacled young woman in the group said, dismissively.

"And what didn't you know about it?" asked the brown haired young woman.

"Why, that there is no such thing as truth. I have always believed otherwise."

"Then you're an—." The young woman stopped. She was going to say "old fool," but thought there was no need to insult such a clueless antique who was likely on the doorstep of death anyway. However, in order to maintain the purity of her ideological commitment in front of her other listeners, she said, "Then you are still living in an imaginary past, probably under false consciousness," she said.

"False consciousness?" Theodore asked.

"Haven't you read a book in the last twenty years, old

man?" the spectacled young woman demanded.

"Well, well, many I should say," the old man—I mean Theodore—said. "But tell me young woman," he continued, turning his attention again to the brown haired speaker, "how did you discover that there is no such thing as truth?"

"Everyone knows it," she said.

"Does that mean that there are no true statements?"

"Yes, it does. There are only subjective opinions."

"Then I am troubled by a lack of understanding. Perhaps you can help me."

"I doubt anyone could help you," one of the young men interjected, his words aimed at Theodore but his eyes looking at the brown haired young woman, possibly to see if he was making points.

"What troubles you, as you put it?" asked the young woman.

"Well," Theodore began, slowly, as if grinding things over in his mind, "you say that there is no such thing as truth and that there are no true statements. Let me see. 'There are no true statements.' Then, if that is correct, it must be incorrect."

"What are you babbling about?" asked the young man.

"The statement, 'There are no true statements,' cannot be a true statement. It must be false by its own claim."

"What I think she means," said one of the young men, rather ostentatiously smoking a pipe, "is that there is no such thing as a single, objective, totalizing truth."

"Don't tell her what she means," sneered the young woman with the spectacles. "That's just like a man."

"I was only going to point out that according to theory, there are many truths, all equal, all true, but none exclusively true."

"I must admit to a poverty of understanding," Theodore said. "For my poor mind cannot grasp how, say, the statements, 'This grass is green,' and 'This grass is brown' can be true at the same time. Can you help me along?"

"Of course," the young man said, in a somewhat condescending tone. "According to theory," he continued, taking a puff on his pipe, "we no longer talk about *either/or*. Instead, we talk about *both/and*."

"So, then, according to some theory you keep mentioning, it's now acceptable to ignore logic and accept contradictions?"

"Logic is a tool of the patriarchy," said the brown haired young woman.

"That's right," said the spectacled young woman. "We don't need truth, logic, or any other tool of oppression. We are truly free to do anything we want."

"As Nietzsche says, 'Since God doesn't exist, anything is possible,'" added the young man with the pipe.

"We make our own way in the world with our own values," agreed the brown haired young woman.

In his heart, Theodore felt rather scandalized that a group of intelligent, young, university students could so cavalierly banish God from his creation. But he thought it best not to show his shock. Instead he asked, "What makes you believe that God does not exist?"

"Science has proved it," said the spectacled young woman.

"Science has proved it?" echoed Theodore, trying to grasp the statement. "Tell, me," he continued, "since science draws its conclusions from experiments, what experiment has proved that God doesn't exist?"

"Um, Earth to old man, get a clue. Read any science book," said the pipe smoker, pausing between puffs to offer his dismissal.

"But," said Theodore, thinking of a new tack, "if all ideas are equally true, then the idea that God doesn't exist and that he does must be equally true."

At this point the other young man, who had been only listening until now made a game-show buzzer sound and said, in a somewhat rude voice, "Thanks for playing."

"Look," said the young man with the pipe, "all truths are equal, but some truths are more equal than others."

"Science is the trump card, old buddy," the other young man said.

"Is there proof of that or is that an assumption?"

Now, these young people were not used to meeting any opposition to their beliefs, however mild the question or challenge. So, this last question from Theodore, added to his others, was the last raindrop that broke the dam.

"You know," the spectacled young woman said, glaring at Theodore, "we were having a private conversation here until you, just like a man, forced your way upon us. We don't have to lie back and let you commit intellectual rape."

"In other words," added the young man with the pipe, "you have outlived your usefulness."

"Where's euthanasia when you need it?" the other young man said.

"As I was saying," said the brown haired young woman, "before we were intruded upon by a textbook example of the old order, truth, like morality, is just a control concept used to manipulate the gullible into behaving according to the power structure's wishes."

Theodore, recognizing that he had been dismissed and was being ignored, gave a slight bow and went on his way. While he didn't exactly repent of his intrusion, neither could it be said that he was either happier or wiser as a result of it.

✠✠✠

FAITH

O nce upon a time, a wicked king attacked a good king's country, in order to conquer and enslave the good king's people. The good king, always anticipating the need to fight evil, called up his forces quickly. The two armies met on a vast battlefield and soon the sound of sword hitting shield—and flesh—reverberated through the sky. The fighting and destruction continued for many days. Sometimes the good king's forces were stronger for a while and pushed back the wicked king's army. Other times the wicked king's forces prevailed and pushed back the good king's forces. But even after many days there was no clear victor, no lasting gain of ground on either side, only the loss of many lives by both armies.

Then one day when the wicked king's forces had made a small advance against the good king's forces, the good king ordered his army to retreat.

"Why are we retreating?" asked the commander of the main unit, "because we are not losing so badly. We can still gain back the ground we have lost."

"The king has so ordered it," replied the general. "And we must trust the king."

But then the king ordered a further retreat and told the army to leave behind its food supplies: its horses and cattle, its wine and cheese, and its flour and its oil.

"Why are we abandoning our much-needed food supplies?" demanded the commander. "This makes no sense. What is the king thinking? He is giving aid to the enemy. They will surely win now."

"The king is wiser than we are," replied the general. "He knows what he's doing. Even when his ways seem strange to us, we must trust him and know that he can see what we cannot see."

As evening approached the commander noticed one of the enlisted men sneaking off toward the enemy camp. As the commander raised his rifle to shoot the deserter, the king came up to him.

"I can get him with one shot before he reaches the ridge," said the commander, beginning to squeeze the trigger in anticipation of the king's acknowledgment.

"Let him go," said the king.

"But sire—" began the commander, who then thought better of it and did not continue his objection. The commander, however, did talk with the general. "I suppose this is another case where must trust the king," he said in a bitter and sarcastic tone.

"Yes," the general replied. "We must always trust him." The commander walked back to his tent shaking his head.

For their meal that night, since they had very little food, the troops were compelled to eat sparsely, sharing a little bread and cheese and—since they had abandoned their wine—some coffee made with the water from a near-by stream. By now the commander kept his thoughts and complaints to himself, but he could not help thinking, "Drinking strong coffee on practically empty stomachs will keep the troops awake all night." Then he thought, "That means we will all be killed in the morning, as we try to fight but are weak from lack of food and sleep." He concluded by muttering aloud to himself, "This is what we get for trusting the king."

About two hours later, it was as the commander predicted. The troops had settled down for the night but were too restless for sleep. The commander himself was wide awake, not from the coffee but from the anxious and resentful thoughts filling his mind.

Suddenly, the adjutant came over and announced that the king had ordered all men to get up and put on their arms. The commander put on his armor quickly and made his way to the general's tent, where he found the general standing next to the king and the deserter.

"All this taken care of," he heard the deserter tell the King. "The sentries will not bother us."

When the king ordered his army to advance to the enemy camp, the commander did not know what to think. He pondered deserting himself, thinking he was walking into an ambush set up by the deserter. But then the deserter was talking to the king. It made no sense. "I hope this makes sense to somebody," he thought.

Soon the army reached the camp of the wicked king, where they found the bodies of the sentries—who had been killed by the "deserter"—and the sound of thousands of men snoring off drunkenness, for the wicked king's army had gorged itself with delight on the food and wine left behind by the good king's orders when his forces retreated.

The good king's army quickly dispatched all the sleeping soldiers of the wicked king's army. The war came to an end, the wicked king retreated to his own land, and peace prevailed throughout the good king's realm.

As the general, the commander, and some fellow officers sat down to one last meal before they all returned to their homes, the general raised his glass in a toast, and said, "This is what we get for trusting the king."

✠✠✠

FAITH AND WORKS

There was once the ruler of a small kingdom who acted as judge for all the disputes in his realm. One day during his usual session, two men came before him.

The first man said, "My neighbor here has stolen my cow, sire. Please give me justice and return it to me."

The king replied, "I certainly believe in justice. However, your neighbor is my friend. Therefore, I rule that the cow belongs to him. Next case."

The next case involved a man accused of stealing a loaf of bread. The man approached the king trembling. "I didn't intend to steal the bread," he said shaking with fear. "It must've fallen into my satchel or the shopkeeper overlooked it when he totaled up my bill. I am an honest man, known in the town for my integrity. I've never been accused of stealing before. Whatever happened, I beg you for mercy."

"Well, I'm certainly a merciful man," the king said. "I believe in kindness and mercy for all my subjects." Then turning to the guards he said, "Take him out, chop off his hands, and deliver him to the torturers."

For the final case, the king's chief accountant was brought before him. "I was looking over your accounts," said the king to him. "And I noticed that you had an addition error."

"I'm so sorry sire," said the accountant. "I will remedy that immediately."

"How do I know you didn't do this on purpose?" demanded the king.

"But sire," answered the accountant. "I have been your accountant for 35 years. Certainly by now you have faith in me."

"Of course I have faith in you," said the king. "Guards, take this man out and hang him."

✠✠✠

FAITH AND REASON

Are you sure you don't want to come back to my place and see my landscapes?" asked Temptation.

"I don't think so," said Reason. "I've got a mountain to climb." Reason tried to stand firm and still, but his legs were being shaken by Weakness and Indecision.

"Another time, perhaps," said Temptation, ever so alluringly.

Reason looked around for Confidence as he tried to shake off Weakness and Indecision, but, to his dismay, he saw that Confidence had joined Pride and both were climbing the Mountain of Error.

Reason, ever convinced of his ability to climb the Mountain of Truth, decided to set about the task by himself. The mountain was daunting and the climb arduous, but after what seemed forever, at the end of a long and thirsty struggle, Reason finally neared the top. But here was a new difficulty. The top jutted out all around the circumference of the mountain, making it impossible to get up over it. Reason looked down and saw Despair mocking him and urging him to jump to his doom. But just then, a slender arm reached over the edge from above and held out a welcoming hand. Reason gladly accepted the offer and with the helper's aid and his own struggling, managed to get over the ledge and up onto the top of the Mountain of Truth.

Imagine Reason's surprise and delight when he saw that his rescuer was a beautiful woman with long, golden hair. "Who are you, " he asked the girl, "and how long have you been here?"

"My name is Faith," answered the girl, "and I have been here all my life."

It was during the time when Faith was explaining to Reason how she had found the way to the top of the Mountain of Truth that the two fell in love and married. Not only did they live happily together, each needing the other, but it so occurred in the natural course of events that a child was born to them whom they named Knowledge.

⌘ *There can be no knowledge without faith joining reason.*[4]

✠✠✠

---

[4] We must have faith in the source of knowledge before we can accept knowledge into our lives. Reason must join with faith because reason alone cannot find knowledge.

ANOTHER QUEST

Only he who befriends Wisdom and Truth will learn how best to climb the mountain of life.
— Proverb

Half a dozen college students decided to spend their spring holiday hiking in the mountains. Being adventurous types, they wanted to hike in an uncommon place, so following their usual hasty decision making style they quickly hit on an obscure (or perhaps imaginary) trail up a series of ever steeper slopes, trekking through the brush and rocks where they thought no one had ever gone. However, after several hours, they struggled over one more ridge and came suddenly upon an old, white-haired man sitting on a ledge overlooking the valley.

"An old man this high up must be a guru," said a young man in a flannel shirt, laughing. "Let's ask him a deep question." And so, since everyone was tired enough and willing to indulge in some recreation, the students all walked over to the man and said hello. The old man made no acknowledgement, in spite of the fact that the sudden appearance of several other people in such a remote area must have been a singular event.

"Tell us, old man," said the young man in the flannel shirt, when the group got closer, "What is the meaning of life?" His tone smacked of mock solemnity.

"Thus are the children of dust mistaken," replied the old man without even looking around to face his interrogator, "for their questions are backwards."

"Ooh, 'children of dust' is good," said a young man with short, black hair, quite amused.

"Backwards, huh?" said the young man in the flannel shirt. "Okay, let's see. What is the meaning of life; life, of, meaning . . . the . . . is, what? Life of meaning the is what? That's forwards?" There was a bit of laughter.

"No, no," said a young man with binoculars, catching on. "It's obvious. The question is, 'What is the life of meaning?' Right, old man?"

"In other words," added a particularly intense young man with short black hair, affecting the pose of a scholar, "you're suggesting that the secret of life lies not in the subscription to a proposition but in the exercise of a methodology." There was a bit of giggling among the others.

As the students had by now walked around to face him, they could see that the old man displayed but the faintest wry smile. "At your place on the path of life," he said, "a question that seeks an explanation of the lives of others is less important than a question whose answer will instruct you yourself how to live."

"This guy's good," said a girl with dark brown hair.

"It is also true," added the old man, "that at this point in your life journey, you are not yet prepared to hear the answer to the first question."

Because they had been trained by their professors to believe that all talk about such philosophical abstractions was "unintelligible verbal noise," without relevance in the contemporary world, the students found quite entertaining someone who seemed to take those ideas seriously.

"Explain yourself," a girl in shorts said, thinking of a line from *Alice in Wonderland* and hoping that the others would get the double meaning.

"To the young," said the old man, "the command, 'Believe me,' is less immediate than the command, 'Follow me.' For what you choose to do is what you choose to believe. Many say they believe one thing but do another."

"So you would concur with the well-known Aristotelian construct that 'action leads to belief,'" said the intense young man with short black hair, still in his professorial pose.

"Action *is* belief," said the old man.

"But how do you reconcile that doctrine," said the young woman in shorts, "with the fact that we sometimes do what we don't want to do, succumbing to temptation or to our weaknesses? We don't always follow the path of wisdom."

"And what is wisdom?" the old man asked in return.

"He doesn't even know what wisdom is?" a girl with glasses asked, with a tone of contemptuous incredulity.

"No, he's right," said a young man with a pair of binoculars. "We need to define wisdom first."

"But that's stupid," said the girl in the shorts. "Everyone knows what wisdom is. Wisdom is knowledge of human nature."

"Well, it's knowledge about people, all right," said the young man wearing a flannel shirt, "but it's more than that. You have to know when to act and when to wait."

"I think wisdom is more like what you learn from experience," said the girl with brown hair. "As you go through life, you learn things that make you tolerant and forgiving, understanding, compassionate. Things happen to you that give you empathy. It's like broadening your outlook."

"But it's not just having experience," said the young man with the binoculars. "You have to analyze what happens to you, to make something of it. I'd define wisdom as analysis of ideas, and maybe generalizing from experience, so you know how to act."

"You guys are just using a lot of words to confuse the issue," said the young man with short black hair. "You talk about when to act and how to act as if there is such a mystery. Wisdom is nothing more than good decision making, and the techniques are now taught in books and classes everywhere. Back in the old days you might have needed a so-called wise man to tell you what to do, but with all the standard tools now available, that time is past. If this guru or whatever he is really knew anything worthwhile, he'd be writing books on business strategy."

The girl with the glasses looked at the young man with the short black hair. "I think your definition is a bit limited," she said. "Wisdom must involve good decision making as you say, but it must be more than just technique. There must be some ability for making good judgments when the situation doesn't lend itself to business school evaluation."

"There aren't any such situations," the young man with the short black hair said. "Haven't you ever heard of subjective linear analysis?"

"But the kind of judgment I mean is for making the right choices when you face moral problems," the girl with the glasses continued. "So wisdom must have some ethical component to it that allows you to discern the true from the false, or even right from wrong."

"But right and wrong are just socially conditioned ideas," said the girl in the shorts.

"And besides, where do we get this discernment except by experience?" asked the girl with the long brown hair. "You live, you make mistakes, you learn."

"The Ghar of Tolul had experience," the old man suddenly interrupted. "He had traveled far, married thirty wives, killed eighty three men, sponsored one thousand feasts, and slept in seven hundred beds, but he was not known as a wise man. He died in a needless war of his own making."

"To become wise you have to know something," said

the young man with the short black hair. "Experience doesn't guarantee knowledge. You have to read a lot of books."

"Many have read two thousand and fourteen books without altering a footstep of their walk or a syllable of their speech," the old man said, as he peered out over the valley below. "Many readers are like travelers who look at everything but see nothing."

"I wonder if he's one of them," whispered the young man in the flannel shirt. "He's not exactly altering his foot-steps."

"So you think reading is worthless?" asked the girl with glasses.

"Whether or not reading has value depends more on the reader than the book," the old man replied. "Although the book is important, too," he added after a brief pause.

"What book or books do you recommend?" two of the students asked at the same time.

"Once again, the children of dust ask questions in the wrong order. The first questions to ask yourself are, Why should I read? What is my purpose for picking up a block of wood and inviting it to speak by opening it? And more importantly, What will I do with what I read?"

"Yes, and you are such a great model of that philoso-phy," said the girl with the glasses, quite sarcastically.

"It's not what you read, but what you remember," said the girl in the shorts. "Whether it comes from books or ex-perience," she added, looking at each of her companions.

"I once knew a man who could remember every meal he had ever eaten, and in remarkable detail," said the old man. "His last words were a mild complaint about a sauce he had been served twenty eight years earlier."

"Okay, old man," said the young man with the binocu-lars. "It's imagination, isn't it? Imagination is the key — the ability to take what you read and see what isn't there."

"My son came to believe that he was an exalted being in charge of the destiny of the earth," said the old man, somewhat softer than before. "He believed that half the world were his slaves and the cther half his would-be assassins. Every day he adjusted the details of monumental battles that only he could see."

"Didn't he realize that he was obviously insane?" asked the young man with the short black hair.

"He did indeed have an extensive knowledge of mental illness," replied the old man, "having studied it at the university before he fell under its curse. And even after he became ill he often accused his imaginary subordinates of being insane, and he named their symptoms with care and detail. But in all his diagnosing, he never applied his knowledge to himself."

"Then wisdom must have something to do with personal insight, with the self-application of knowledge," said the girl with glasses.

"Of course," said the young man with the binoculars. "If you don't make use of knowledge, what good is it?"

"Look," said the young man with short black hair, "talk like this never goes anywhere. All you need to do is distinguish between what is important and what is not important."

"Do not burglars and gluttons, misers and egotists — and even the slothful all believe they do exactly that?" asked the old man, looking briefly at the group of young people for the first time.

"Well, of course, we're talking about normal, rational people," said the young man in the flannel shirt.

"Who can make good judgments, based on meaningful values," added the girl with long brown hair, completing her fellow student's sentence.

"But who decides what meaningful values are?" asked the young man with the binoculars.

"Tell us, old man," said the young man in the flannel shirt, "what is this life of meaning you were on about?"

"Life is a quest," said the old man, causing two or three of the students to nudge each other and exchange knowing looks before framing their faces with artificially attentive expressions. "A quest for purpose, a reason to get up in the morning, to act, to work. Behind this lies the need to find meaning. Behind meaning lies interpretation."

"Yeah, I've heard that famous saying, 'The central work of life is interpretation,'" said the girl with glasses.

"So you are near the path," said the old man.

"Only near?"

"To travel the path, you must find truth."

"Oh, now we're on a really clear subject," said the young man with the short black hair, sarcastically. "We should have that sewn up in no time." Then, not receiving an immediate response, he added, "Do you guys know that it will be dark in a few hours and we have to go back down the same rocky, bushy way we came up, only maybe with the addition of snakes? And besides, I'm already getting hungry."

The reference to snakes immediately got the girls' attention. "Snakes? You're joking," said the girl in shorts.

"Let's get going now," said the girl with the long brown hair.

"Are there really snakes around here?" the girl with glasses asked the old man.

"I have met with some," he answered.

"Wait," said the young man with the binoculars. "Did we ever decide on what wisdom is?"

"Who cares about wisdom?" the young woman in shorts said, quite intensely. "Let's get out of here while it's still light. I don't want to step on a snake in the dark."

"I forgot what we said," the young man in the flannel shirt said in answer to the previous question.

"Maybe wisdom is being able to remember what you've learned," mused the young man with the binoculars.

As the students began to pick up their water bottles, walking sticks, and other assorted hiking gear, the young man with the short black hair said to his companions, "You guys are as bad as Plato—raising meaningless questions and then playing with even more meaningless abstract arguments over mere words only to arrive in the air. And this guru ought to imitate Socrates."

"You mean, he should ask more questions?" the young man in the flannel shirt asked.

"No. I mean that he should try some hemlock."

Just as they were heading toward the path by which they had arrived, the old man said, in a voice not much louder than his conversational tone, "You have neglected to ask one final question."

"I don't care what it is," said the young woman in shorts.

"Come on, let's go," said the young man with the short black hair.

The young man with the binoculars, being at the end of the line of the group as they were entering the narrow path back down the mountain, turned around and said, "Okay, what is that question?"

"The question is, 'Is there an easier way down the mountain?'"

"Hey wait," the young man shouted to his companions. Then to the old man, he asked, "Okay, is there an easier way down the mountain?"

"Yes," replied the old man. "Across this clearing and down a short trail, you will come to a road. Go down that road a hundred yards and you will find a bus stop. There is a bus every two hours. It will take you down the mountain."

"Thank you so much, old man," the young man said. "I don't know how to thank you."

"Thanks are not necessary," replied the old man. "I get my reward when I can teach someone about wisdom and truth, as I have just done for you."

"But—" the young man began, about to object. He stopped, however, when he realized that the old man was right.

✠✠✠

A Conversation about "Another Quest"[5]

Half a dozen college students sat around the table in a coffee shop near the Theater Department at a large university. They were discussing a story that each had recently appeared in.

"That's the dumbest story I've ever been in," said a young woman with glasses. "I mean, no plot, no action, just a bunch of lame dialog."

"You had a decent part," a young woman in shorts said. "But he puts me in shorts and then uses that to describe me. Not my hair, not my wit, not my major. Just shorts. So all a reader will do is think about my legs. As if I'm some sort of gratuitous sex object."

"What about me?" a young man with short black hair said. "He makes me out to be some fake poser type, pretending to be a pseudointellectual, who has read Plato and Aristotle, and at any rate is a pompous idiot."

"I like the way he referred to me as the girl with long brown hair," said a young woman—with long, brown hair. "And I got to play a gentle and compassionate girl."

"Look," said a young man wearing a flannel shirt, "it was work. We needed the money. It doesn't matter that I don't believe—or even understand—a word of what I spoke."

"And what the heck is the point of the story?" asked the young woman with glasses. "Are we supposed to get some meaning out of it? That wasn't just lame dialog. It was opaque dialog."

---

[5] A modest contribution to metafiction.

"It means whatever you want it to mean," said the young man with short black hair. "That's the trouble with fiction."

"So then it means that strawberries are cheaper than cherries on alternate Tuesdays," the girl in glasses said sarcastically.

"I think the trip up and down the mountain is a metaphor for the journey of life, " said a young man, just placing a pair of binoculars on the table. "When you learn truth and are then able to apply wisdom, the journey is a lot easier, because you discover the paths that others have carved out successfully."

"Ooh, a wise man," said the young man with short black hair. "Need a mountain to sit on?"

"I still don't get it," said the young woman in shorts.

"Anyway," said the young man with short black hair, changing the subject. "Do any you guys have a copy of the upcoming ethics midterm? I need to study."

✠✠✠

YOU LOOK, BUT YOU DO NOT SEE

Once upon a time, possibly even during your own lifetime, a young man decided to be different and search for wisdom instead of pleasure. (I know, I know, but bear with me. It's just a story.) So, one fine morning, he locked the front door of his house and began a walk down the street.

The first person he met had the look of a man who had taken too many shortcuts. "Go full speed, get as much as you can, and don't look back," was his advice. "You've got to move fast enough to keep ahead of the flames, the explosions, and the jealous husbands." He then hot-wired a nearby car and sped off the wrong way down a one-way street, hitting a few trash cans and swerving to avoid a head-on collision with another car.

The young man decided that he needed more than only one recommendation to choose from, and he also felt uncertain about the connection between the shortcutter's advice and true wisdom. So he continued on his search.

The next person he met was a middle aged woman who ran a small variety shop with a few grocery items in the downtown area. "Wisdom," she said after thinking for a few moments, "is nothing more than going with the flow. Follow what others do, read the books they read, watch the movies the watch, and you'll do fine, always participating in the middle of things. Go along to get along. That's wisdom in a nutshell."

The young man was very impressed with this advice, so he made a purchase at the woman's store: he bought a dozen eggs. However, after he had gone a few blocks, he decided to check his purchase. In the egg carton were only eleven eggs and two of them were broken. He also noticed for the first time that she had shortchanged him.

"I'm not so sure I should take the advice of someone whose character appears to be so compromised," he thought. "Though, of course, she might talk better than she lives, and her advice might be sound." But the young man continued his search, in any event.

The next person he met was a tired looking old man, who recommended slowing down. "Stop and look around. Wisdom is like beauty: it is everywhere, if only you will look for it."

"I don't understand," said the young man.

"Suppose you drive through a mountain pass and look at the grandeur of nature. Those who do not know how to look will say, 'Rocks and trees. So what?' But those who ask, 'What is here that is beautiful?' will discover grandeur and majesty and awe inspiring vistas. The same is true with wisdom. Many people live lives without understanding. They learn little from experience because they look, but they do not see. But the world, both in nature and in artifice, reveals itself deeply to those who know how to open their eyes."

"Teach me how to open my eyes," the young man said, curious about the old man's thinking.

"Look over at that field. What do you see?"

"Rolls of hay."

"Yes. But I also see symbols of potential. You can feed a good horse or a bad horse. Potentials can be used for good or ill. A pot of stew will feed a good man or a bad man. Take thought about how potential will be used. Hay represents energy, whether it's fed to a horse so that it will have strength to plow or burned in a brick oven to bake bread. And it represents comfort for animals who need a bed softer than the earth."

"And it could stuff a scarecrow to protect a field," added the young man.

"Yes," affirmed the old man. "Good. Now look at that vacant lot. What do you see there?"

"A bunch of trash. Or maybe could it be a symbol of the carelessness of our society? People are just thoughtless about tossing their junk everywhere."

"You are correct," said the old man, "but to discover the deepest wisdom, you must continue to think. For example, in this trash, which others might dismiss as merely junk and not give it a second thought as they walk by, we can see the limits of material happiness, the detritus of human aspiration, the slag of choice, the shards of the heart, the relics of long forgotten dreams, the ephemera of purchased hopes, the future of greed, a sampling of the history of technology, a forewarning against putting one's soul into possessions."

"That's amazing," the young man said, with awe.

"There is much more. Do you not see here an emblem of transactional love? For when something—and often someone—becomes no longer useful, do we not banish it from our lives with barely a thought and choose another? For we are a disposable society, one that has been trained by our culture to buy, consume, and throw away. And here you see the universal transitoriness of everything new—the consequences of the hunger for novelty, which causes too many to attempt in futility to fill the emptiness in their souls, the shallowness of the heart that grows bored easily and wants something always new. New wristwatch, new shoes, new automobile, new house, new values, new spouse, new truth."

"I never knew such meaning could be hidden in a trash-covered vacant lot," said the young man, gazing over the lot and trying to notice every empty beer can, bicycle wheel, and piece of rusty metal. "And I bet every individual item could mean something, too."

"Yes, it could," replied the old man. "Every piece of trash has a story. And every piece of trash can represent something else. That's how we deal with metaphors and the symbols we find in art. But in all your symbolizing, do not let your eyes be so obsessed with some things that you do not see the others."

"Okay, what?" asked the young man, peering even more intently so he would not miss anything.

"We haven't even begun to discuss the weeds," replied the old man.

✠✠✠

THE FAIR

Early on the day after the fair had closed, a few men labored under an overcast sky to dismantle the rides. Several spokes were already missing from the Ferris wheel, much of the Octopus Whirl rested heavily on the grass, and the roller coaster was now a barren track showing gaps in the rails.

The distant whirr of the riding sweepers reflected across the huge but empty parking lot as they vacuumed up the discarded memories of the night before.

As a truck pulled away with a load of disassembled game booths piled on its bed, one worker looked down at the grass where he noticed a few pieces of a ticket, a smashed toy car, and the shriveled skin of a burst balloon.

"Only the ghost of imagination is left," he thought. "The experiences of the previous night have vanished even as they occurred. And this litter here, the detritus of enjoyment, is the only evidence that anything at all ever happened."

But in a thousand bedrooms not far from the fairgrounds, a thousand children were even now awaking, with smiles on their faces and laughter in their hearts.

✠✠✠

[NEEDS A TITLE]

Once there was a man who wrote stories—when he could get around to it, but something always seemed to come up that caused him once again to put off writing. [Revise this part soon.] He had many ideas, such as [put some examples here], but he couldn't seem to make the time to develop them because [put some excuses here about planning and procrastination].

"Someday," he promised himself, "I will sit down and write." But Tuesday, not Someday, came after Monday; and Wednesday, not Someday, came after Tuesday. And so it was throughout the week. [Put in witty but solid ending statements here.]

[Think of a moral for this.]

✠✠✠

THE CONCERT

B iff had liked Molly for a long time. He liked the way she behaved so generously toward others, how she spoke in such a warm and friendly way to everyone, and how she knew so much about life. But Biff had never been able to think of an excuse to just sit down and talk to her. Communication seemed so difficult. Eager to try anything, Biff asked himself, "Where can I take her that will provide her with enjoyment at the same time that we can talk and get to know each other better?"

Movies were out. "Movies are a wasted date," Biff thought, "because you sit together in the dark and to please your date you watch some chick flick where people act awkward and mushy and there isn't even a single exploding helicopter or collapsing building. Nope," he concluded, "movies have no opportunity for communication."

Lunch was out, also. Too informal, and not enough time to talk about each other. "My mouth is always full of sandwich or burrito or turkey leg," he said to himself. "And, besides, Mom always told me it's not polite to talk with your mouth full."

Same with just going for coffee, although if Molly resisted any other proposal, going for coffee would be better than nothing. "And there's the minor issue that I don't like coffee or tea," Biff thought.

Finally, Biff decided to ask Molly to go with him to a rock concert. "Concerts are usually several hours long," he thought, "and that should allow plenty of time to talk things over and at the same time enjoy the music."

After a little research, to his delight, Biff found out that there was a live concert in the local arena Saturday night. Rejoicing in his good fortune, Biff ran to Molly's house and asked her to go. Happily, she agreed.

On Saturday, the concertgoers were streaming into the arena well ahead of time, and soon there was standing room only.

To hurry this story along, let's say that the first set came on stage. The band was called, "Death Metaphor." Just as Biff was apologizing to Molly for being unable to get seats closer to the stage, the first wham of the drums shot from the multiple, huge speakers and staggered many people, knocking several to the ground.

Then the band began its first song. The speakers created such a sound pulse with every beat, that the hearts of the audience members were instantly synchronized with the song's percussive rhythm. Many in the audience began to cough as the rhythm pounded on their chests.

The guitars were amplified to such an extent that the chords zinging out of the instruments began to vibrate the wax out of the hearers' ears. Then the guitar leader slammed into an extended riff that not only melted any remaining ear wax, but drained the listeners' sinuses, too.

"How do you like it?" Biff yelled at Molly.

"Yes, I've seen cows when I go hiking," Molly yelled back. "Why?"

"Yeah, I know the price was sky high, but it was worth it to be with you!" screamed Biff.

"Pridefully Sly Worms? Is that the next group?"

"We're communicating!" Biff thought, joyfully.

After just a few minutes, the audience had been rendered nearly deaf and was experiencing the concert mostly through the powerful vibrations and body slams punched out by the sound system.

Then the opening band left and the headliner band came on stage. The "Tombstone Synopsis" turned up the

volume and began banging out spine drilling, tooth loos-
ening noise accompanied by unintelligible lyrics screamed
into the microphone. It wasn't long before several people
ran from the arena yelling in pain. Several others had lost
consciousness and collapsed onto the floor.

When the drummer hit all his drums at once as hard as
he could, the huge speakers blew out in one final distort-
ed, spark-filled punch, knocking more than half of the audience over. The amplifiers arced, circuit breakers snapped
off, and the arena was cast into a deep, silent darkness.

None of those who were still conscious could hear the
sirens as the ambulances approached, and few were aware
that they were being picked up and transported, or that
blood was running out of their ears.

Six weeks later, Biff and McIly had recovered some of
their hearing, so they were able to talk—or rather, yell—to
each other.

"Great concert, huh?" yelled Biff.

"What did you say?" Molly yelled back.

"No, six weeks ago yesterday," Biff yelled, louder.

"Who's going to fix what leaks that are yet to die?"
screamed Molly, confused.

"Did you like the concert?" Biff screamed back.

"No, I don't ride a bike on dirt," Molly screamed so
loud that it made her hoarse.

So Biff decided to write a note. "Did you like the concert?" he wrote.

Molly wrote back, "The one last week? No. The volume
was so low I could hardly hear the music. Not like the one
we went to six weeks ago. It was awesome." As she
pushed the note toward him, their hands touched.

Biff looked at Molly and read an unspoken message in
her eyes. He smiled, glad that he could finally communicate with her.

✠✠✠

CULTURE

A t one point in time in one land so far away, there lived a man who was completely virtuous. This would have been a good thing, of course, except that in this land, no one else was like him. Everyone else viewed him with suspicion.

"What's he up to?" someone would ask.

"I know he's working some angle," another would say.

Once when a neighbor ran short of grain for his cattle, he came to the virtuous man to buy what he lacked. "I need 30 bushels," the neighbor said. So the virtuous man carefully measured out 30 bushels and gave them to the neighbor. When the neighbor got back to his farm, he measured the grain. It was just over 30 bushels. The farmer looked through the grain. There was no dirt or rocks. He counted his change. It was exact. "Why, that poor slob doesn't even know how to cheat," thought the neighbor, with contempt. Then he had a horrifying thought: "Maybe he's poisoned the grain." But it wasn't so.

Another neighbor's cow got loose and strayed into the virtuous man's grazing area, where the grass was much tastier. When the neighbor followed the tracks of his cow, he reached the virtuous man's field. "That's a mighty fine cow you have there," said the neighbor.

"What?" said the virtuous man. "That's not my cow. I wonder where it came from."

"Are you sure it isn't your cow?" asked the neighbor. "It sure looks at home."

"No, no. It must belong to a neighbor. Will you help me find the rightful owner?"

As he led his cow home, the neighbor thought to himself, "That guy is such a loser. Why, he can't even lie when it could gain him a nice cow."

The virtuous man's reputation spread throughout the area. At the town hall meetings, he was mockingly addressed as "Mr. Morality," "Dr. Perfect," and "The Vicar of Virtue." It wasn't too many months before the man began to think of his virtue as a defect, for it had so separated him from his fellow citizens, and it was so contrary to the behavior of everyone else.

Then one day he overheard his young daughter talking to her mother. "Mommy," the little girl said, "teach me how to lie, cheat, and steal. All the other kids know how."

"Why, of course, darling," the little girl's mother replied.

The virtuous man felt his knees weaken. Was truth, integrity, virtue such a bad thing? He called to his wife. "My darling," he said, "I heard you promise our daughter that you would teach her how to be dishonest."

"You must be mistaken, my husband," his wife replied. "I would no more teach her how to lie than I would be unfaithful to you."

"You're right," said the virtuous man. "If I can't trust my wife to be honest, I myself would not only be living a lie, but I would be bereft of a soul mate and forced to pass through life alone, even though surrounded by a wife and children."

"You are right, as always," his wife replied.

Something in his wife's manner persuaded the man that a life of simple honesty was better than a life of calculated duplicity. So, even at the cost of love and friendship, he continued to live as a contrarian in the land.

✠✠✠

Writing Your Life

A man who had been a lifelong student of wisdom had compiled a book of axioms, advice, and analysis, a book he called, *1000 Sayings for Life*. He had copies made and presented them to his young sons and daughters. To his dismay, his children refused to read it after leafing through a few pages.

Not willing to give up on training his children to love knowledge and to practice wisdom, the man told his children, "Because it is obvious that you have no desire to learn wisdom from old folks, you shall learn from yourselves. Each night before you go to bed, you must write down one idea that was important that day."

"What do you mean?" his children asked, in a tone that expressed their hostility toward the idea.

"Each day," explained their father, "write down one thing you have learned, such as a generalization about human nature or life, or a criticism of generalizations. Write what you have learned, good and bad, from your life experience.

"Do we have to?" asked one child.

"Yes," said the father. "Since you are unwilling to learn from my mistakes, you will learn from your own—and make note of it for future reference."

"What if we can't think of anything?"

"Answering that question is a critical one, for to ask it implies a poverty of human interpretation. You should always be able to think of something."

At first, the children worked perfunctorily on the task, often writing nominal sentences ("Today I learned that I still like chocolate ice cream") and sometimes including personal comments ("Today I learned that Mommy and Daddy yell and break things when they get mad, and it frightens me).

As they got older, their entries became more philosophical. For example, "Today I learned never to compare one woman with another when either one is present," or "Today I learned that asking for someone's permission to do something, even though you don't need to, makes that person feel very good — because they feel important."

Many years later, their father died and left the children his estate, which included his own book of thoughts. Now in late maturity, they opened their father's book with delight and read it profitably. "I wish we had read and known this stuff when we were younger," one of them said.

"I know what you mean," said another. "We could have avoided so many wrong choices and poor decisions."

"Yes, and it seems that our kids are as stubborn as we were," added a third. "I've tried, without success, to have my own children read both my journal and father's.

"They want to make their own mistakes."

"Well, as long as they record them and tell what solutions they tried and with what results, that's the important part. And perhaps their children will break the mold and learn some wisdom by reading."

Not long after this, a visiting relative asked the father's children, "Aren't you glad that you don't have to continue to write down a thought every day now that your father isn't here to make you?"

"Oh, we all still continue," the children all agreed.

"But why?" asked the relative. "You're adults now, and most likely you have little left to learn about wisdom or whatever it is you put in your books."

"With a little thought," answered the eldest child, "you can learn wisdom until the day you die. I find it easier than ever to make an entry — or two or three — every day."

"But for me, the most important part," said the youngest child, "is that I've learned to pay attention to the meaning of life, to seek out the meaning in everything — every event, observation, experience, every person I meet."

"Every person?" asked the relative. "Am I to conclude that I will be in your book?"

"I've already made an entry from what I've learned from you?"

"Really? What have you learned?"

"The entry will be, 'Belief must precede knowledge, because you are unlikely to discover knowledge that you don't believe can exist.' For example, if you believe that there is no wisdom to be learned, you're going to miss a lot of it."

"You got all that from talking to me?" the relative asked, incredulously.

"Yes. I've trained myself to look for meaning."

"But is it possible for everything to have a meaning?"

"You'd be surprised how much richer, deeper, and satisfying life is when you ask of everything, 'What does this mean?' or 'What lesson does this teach?'"

"I'd rather spend my time savoring a perfectly cooked oh-so-delicious steak, or even reading a good book, to put it in terms of something your type values. Looking for wisdom just to write it down and then forget it seems like such a bore. No offense, but frankly, who cares about meaning? Let's just enjoy ourselves."

"Ah," said the youngest, "another entry."

"Which is?"

"'Some people prefer experience over meaning in life.' You see how easy this is? All you need to do is care, be alert, think, and be intentional about it."

"I think I care about intentionally being alert to seek a piece of chocolate cake," the relative said, and then began looking around the room as if in search for just that.

✠✠✠

CREATION

Once upon a time, a rather severe government hired a talented architect to design an enormous theme park that would tell the history of the nation.

The architect set out on his task, using the design and build model, where parts of the park were built while others were still being designed. This approach allowed the park to be completed in six years, complete not only with miniature representations of factories, cities, roads, and houses, but with beautiful models of forests, lakes, beaches, grasslands, mountains, and wildlife.

The park proved enormously popular and attracted many visitors, who praised the artistry of the designer. "The flowers are so realistic," they said.

"And I expect that sheep to bleat at any moment," others said admiringly.

But then, at a state dinner, where the architect had finished a third glass of wine, he accidentally let a comment slip out that was interpreted as being critical of the regime.

The next day, the architect was nowhere to be seen. Soon, his name was removed from the plaque in front of the park, brochures and state histories were reprinted with his name removed, and all historical photographs were retouched to remove his image.

The park remained in operation, as beautiful as ever. One day some foreign dignitaries were invited to visit the park, and they were delighted. They spent many hours looking around and taking pictures.

Finally, one of them said, "This place is just a wonder of artistic ability. Who designed it?"

The question clearly presented a problem for the state, since it had taken such pains to eliminate all reference to the architect. However, when the architect fell from favor, the bureaucrats had formulated an answer to be given whenever a foreigner might ask. (No citizen would ever ask, the people having long ago discovered the penalty for doing so.)

"Yes, yes," a fellow foreign dignitary said, "we must know who designed this beautiful and elegant park."

"No one," said the government tour guide.

"No one? What do you mean? That it just happened?"

"Yes."

"But it shows such intelligence, creativity, beauty, uniqueness. What's this about 'No one'? Come now and tell us who made this beautiful world."

"Our next stop," said the tour guide, "is the Museum of Victory Over the Aggressors."

✠✠✠

THE LAST VALENTINE

Here it is, said the man,
 The last one this old press
 Will ever print.
Seems it ought to be special—
Maybe we should frame it—
But business is business.
Here, put it in the box
And send it off
Where someone will buy it,
And use it to mark a beginning
Rather than an end.

✠✠✠

ABOUT THE AUTHOR

Robert Harris was born in 1950 in Los Angeles, California. He grew up in Inglewood in a house made of adobe bricks, built by his father. In 1960 the family moved to several empty and somewhat isolated acres on the outskirts of Corona, California. There, in the absence of other children to play with, he and his brother invented imaginary cities (complete with drive-in wide-screen theaters) and people (including avatars of their own personalities).

All through his higher education, he majored in English, eventually obtaining a PhD from the University of California. He taught English, together with a few courses in critical thinking and creative thinking, at the college and university level for many years.

He later worked as an instructional designer in the world of corporate training. Now, he is allegedly retired, allowing him time to write more stories.

Dr. Harris now lives in Tustin, California with his wife, Marie.

Please visit the author's Web site at
www.virtualsalt.com

Colophon
Set in Book Antiqua
12 point
&

LUCIDA SANS
12 point bold small caps